Heal Me

COOPERS CREEK # 2

BRONWEN EVANS

All rights reserved. No part of this publication may be reproduced, distributed or transmitted in any form or by any means, including photocopying, recording, or other electronic or mechanical methods, without the prior written permission of the publisher, except in the case of brief quotations embodied in critical reviews and certain other noncommercial uses permitted by copyright law.

For permission requests, write to the publisher, addressed "Attention: Permissions Coordinator," at the address below.

Bronwen Evans/NYLA Publishing
PO Box 8656, Havelock North, New Zealand.
www.bronwenevans.com

Heal Me
Copyright © 2017 by Bronwen Evans
Excerpt From: Bronwen Evans. "Want Me." Copyright © 2017
ISBN-13: 978-1542993302
ISBN-10: 154299330X

ALL RIGHTS RESERVED.

Publisher's Note: This is a work of fiction. Names, characters, places, and incidents are a product of the author's imagination. Locales and public names are sometimes used for atmospheric purposes. Any resemblance to actual people, living or dead, or to businesses, companies, events, institutions, or locales is completely coincidental.

Dedication

To Robin Deeter, you know why.

Acknowledgement

I love my job. Yip, I call it a job because I make my living from writing. However, I rarely think of it as a job, except on those days where the words won't come. Then I curse, stomp around a bit, and then take Brandy and Duke for a walk to clear my head and let my characters talk to me.

It's the greatest job in the world and the hardest job too. But I wouldn't want to do anything else.

So, dear readers, thank you.
Read. Feel. Fall in Love.

"Romance novels…They're fairy tales for grown-ups."
― Gena Showalter, *The Darkest Night*

Chapter One

"Hang on! I'm coming!"

Ric added a curse under his breath. He hated these bloody crutches. As slow as a hobbled horse, Ric swung his way to the front door as fast as his mastery of the crutches would allow. Reaching it, he yanked it open and stared into a gorgeous pair of chocolate-brown eyes, the painful path to the door forgotten.

"Dr. Donoghue?" Well, hell yes! Sexy vet. He almost wanted to buy a dog himself.

"Yes. You must be Ric Stanford, Emily's brother."

The woman's beauty rendered him mute for a moment. Then he mentally shook himself and smiled. "Yeah. Sorry it took me so long to get to the door. I had to dodge around Coco's, uh, accidents."

He moved back to allow her entry into the house.

"That's okay. You can just call me Kate," she said. "Where is she?"

"I penned her in the laundry room so that she didn't keep puking all over the place. It's this way. Just watch out for landmines."

As he led her through the living room and dining room, Ric was careful not to catch one of his crutches on anything. Clumsy and crutches went hand in hand, not the image he wanted in front of this beauty.

"Don't worry about me. I'm used to dealing with that sort of stuff. Occupational hazard and all that," Kate said.

Ric smiled. "I just didn't want you to slip and fall on dog crap. One of us on crutches is enough. I really appreciate you making a house call like this. I still can't reach Emily. Her phone must've died and I can't drive since I'm on pain meds."

"You did the right thing calling me. A first puppy is special and your niece, Hayley loves Coco so much."

As they reached the kitchen, Ric stopped and grimaced at the small pile of dog poop on the hardwood floor. "Damn, that reeks."

Having grown up riding and taking care of horses, Ric could handle the smell of shit, but Coco's stank worse than anything he'd ever encountered before.

Kate sat her bag on the kitchen table and took out some Latex gloves. "Believe it or not, I've smelled worse."

"You're kidding?"

Kate's shook her head a little and smiled. Ric noted that her pink, Cupid's bow lips were devoid of lipstick or gloss. It didn't look like she wore makeup at all. However, Kate wasn't in need of cosmetics to enhance her natural beauty.

Rich, chestnut-brown hair hung down past her shoulders and thick, black lashes framed her dark eyes. High cheekbones, a straight, pretty nose, and a lightly tanned complexion combined to create one of the most arresting female faces that Ric had ever seen.

"I'm going to collect a sample so I can do a culture back at the clinic."

"Okay."

Ric watched her take out a collection kit. She crouched down in front of him and Ric took advantage of the opportunity to check her out. Her light blue jeans were faded and there was a ragged tear in the right knee. She wore beat-up tan cowboy boots and a red-and-black heavy men's flannel jacket. The jeans fit her like a glove, showing off her shapely legs and heart-shaped ass. A tomboy. A very *sexy* tomboy.

I wouldn't mind climbing into the hayloft with her. He snapped his gaze away from her as she stood up, instead looking at the clock on the wall.

"Where's the laundry room?" Kate asked as she deposited her specimen in a Ziploc bag and shut it.

"Right through here." He hobbled through a doorway and down a short hallway. Putting a hand on the doorknob, he said, "I don't know what we're going to find."

Kate laughed. "You make it sound like a murder scene."

The slightly throaty sound and her sparkling eyes sent a jolt of awareness through Ric and he smiled back as he opened the door. Coco, a chocolate Spoodle puppy, bounded out of the laundry room, catching him off-guard when she jumped up at him.

Four months old now, Coco was growing rapidly and she was strong. One of Ric's crutches slid out from under him and he fell back against the wall. It jarred his broken ankle, sending pain lancing through the offended joint.

"Fuck!"

Kate grabbed his left arm to help steady him.

Coco was oblivious to Ric's plight and wagged her tail furiously as she sniffed Kate's legs.

"Are you okay?" Kate asked, meeting his eyes.

Ric stood six-two and he judged Kate to be around five-eight or five-nine; tall for a woman. Her grip on his bicep was firm and her hands were strong, yet feminine. She smelled like hay, horse, and lilac. Hunger stole through him as he glanced at her full lips. It had been a few weeks without a woman and Kate was causing his libido to dance in delighted want and need.

Realizing that she was expecting an answer, Ric pulled it together. "Yeah. I'll live."

She didn't move and their eyes locked for a few moments. Then she seemed to come back to herself with a start. "I'll get your crutch."

Before she bent to retrieve it, Ric saw that she was blushing and smiled to himself. Either his pain meds were making him loopy or they'd shared a moment of mutual attraction. He hoped it was the latter.

"Are you sure that you're all right?" she asked as she handed him the crutch.

"Yeah. I'm just glad there was a wall there. It's the strangest thing." He smiled self-deprecatingly. "You'd think a champion roper would have more coordination on these things. I guess I need more practice."

Kate's mouth curved upwards in response to his smile. A dimple in her right cheek winked at him and he was fascinated by it. "Take your time. You don't need to break anything else. I'll examine Coco in the kitchen. Why don't you go sit down? There's really nothing you can do to help me."

"You sure?"

Kate nodded. "Positive. I'll hold Coco until you get settled."

"Thanks."

Ric's ankle throbbed as he carefully made his way to the living room. He felt bad for leaving Kate to deal with Coco, but she was a veterinarian, so she was used to subduing excited animals. He went over to the recliner he'd been set up in and sat down in it. Some of the pain in his ankle was alleviated when he raised the footrest.

A bottle of hydrocodone sat on the stand by the chair. Ric hated taking the pain meds, but the two fractures hurt like a bitch at times and the drug at least took the edge off and helped him sleep. Sighing, he took two out of the bottle and took them with the homemade lemonade Emily had left him early that afternoon.

He heard Kate talking to Coco out in the kitchen. The slightly smoky timber of her voice was pleasant to the ear and she had a great laugh. Did she have a boyfriend? Was she married? He hadn't noticed if she wore a ring. Although he might be a womanizer, Ric was no homewrecker.

Secretly a romantic, he firmly believed in fidelity and wouldn't even think of getting involved with someone who was in a committed relationship. After seeing how happy his sister and her husband Tyler were, Ric had been thinking more about settling down himself. He loved his niece, Hayley, to death and he wanted a whole passel of kids of his own. Trouble was, finding the right women. He knew the pain that came of bad choices. He'd loved a woman once who'd led him a merry dance. When he finally gave up on her, she got herself killed and he still wondered if he could have done more...If somehow he might have saved her.

Kate was definitely not a 'wildcat,' the type of women his sister accused him of dating to protect himself from hurt. She'd pointed out that he'd never fall in love with that sort of woman.

While he definitely found the sexy vet attractive, he instinctively knew she was not the type of woman who indulged in one-night stands, and he definitely wasn't sure he was ready for more just yet. He was enjoying New York. Enjoying the fast pace of the investment world and the respected place his firm, Horizon Enterprises, held in it.

Kate was the type of woman Emily would try to fix him up with. If Emily didn't love this puppy so much he'd almost imagine her setting this scenario up.

His morose musings were interrupted by Kate's reappearance. "Well, the good news is that Coco will be fine."

"What about the blood in her poop?"

Kate cocked her head. "Are there any trashcans around that Coco can get into?"

Ric gave her a startled look. "Yeah. All over the house. Uh oh. Are you saying she's eaten something she shouldn't? What did she eat?"

"I'm not sure, but it caused some inflammation. Most likely, the worst is over. I palpated her abdomen, but it wasn't tender. Her temperature was normal, too. I'll let Emily know the culture results, but I think she just got into something she shouldn't have. Just try to keep her out of the waste cans," Kate replied.

"You can see I'm on crutches. Keeping Coco from doing

anything at the moment is a bit tricky."

Kate laughed and the sound went straight to his groin. He wished he could cross his legs. "Perhaps until you're healed, keep the bins out of her reach."

Ric's vision was starting to get fuzzy. The damn pills were kicking in already. "All right. I'll make sure to tell Emily and Tyler. I guess we'll have to make sure that our bedroom doors are shut. I appreciate you coming over like this."

She smiled and Ric's stomach did a funny little flip. "I don't mind. I was at the Jones's farm. Jack wanted me to be there while he was breeding someone's mare to Prince Phillip."

Ric smiled. "He still has him, huh? We always busted Jack's ass about that name. No Quarter horse stallion should be named Prince Phillip." His eyes were growing heavier by the second and he shook his head to clear it. "I'm sorry. I don't usually fall asleep when a beautiful woman is talking to me. It's the meds."

She laughed, her cheeks turning pink. "Thank you. Well, I should go and let you get some rest. Do you want me to put Coco in her crate?"

Ric nodded. "That would be great. Thanks."

Her smile was the last thing he remembered as he lost the battle to stay awake.

*****

When his eyes drifted shut, Kate couldn't help watching him for a few moments. His slightly unruly hair and relaxed expression were adorable. She took a lap afghan from the back of the couch and covered him with it.

Even in sleep, the man exuded a potent masculinity and

Kate fought the urge to kiss him. Her heart suddenly knocked against her ribs and she hurriedly moved away from him before she did something stupid.

Get a grip, Kate admonished herself. When she'd steadied him in the laundry, grabbing his rock-hard bicep shouldn't have affected her so much, but she hadn't touched muscles like that in almost two years. Not since her fiancé died. She had to admit that Ric was one fine piece of man-candy. The first man, since arriving in Coopers Creek almost eighteen months ago, who made her feel—anything. With cobalt blue eyes, sandy blond hair, and a sculpted body built for sin, he was temptation personified.

Kate's insides clenched. She hadn't been attracted to a man in a long time, but there was no denying the spark she'd shared with Ric. *Just because it's there doesn't mean you have to act on it.*

Although she'd tried not to notice Ric's scrumptious body as he'd left the kitchen, it proved impossible. His wide shoulders worked under his T-shirt, his muscles bunching and flexing as he moved. Kate had a vivid image of all that sexiness naked and in her bed.

She took a step back. Where the hell had that thought come from?

Kate sucked in a breath and tore her thoughts away from that topic. She was supposed to be tending to a sick puppy, not fantasizing about a man, no matter how hot he was. Focusing on her job, she called Coco to her and put her in her crate in the laundry room.

Back in the kitchen, she found cleaning supplies under the sink and took care of Coco's four messes. Then she checked on Ric, who was sound asleep. Again, she had the crazy impulse to kiss his sensual mouth.

Getting a hold of herself, Kate left the living room, gathered her bag, and left. As she drove down the road, she couldn't get Ric out of her head. It had been a long time since a man had affected her like that and it scared the hell out of her. The pain of loss had finally been easing, but now it reemerged with a vengeance. She forced herself to think about all the work waiting for her back at the clinic, determined to erase the memory of Mr. Tall, Blond and Hot from her brain.

Chapter Two

"I'm fine, Emily! Stop bugging me," Ric snapped at his sister, Emily Jeffries.

She narrowed her hazel eyes at him. "I'm just trying to make sure you have everything you need before I take Hayley to school."

Ric sighed and rubbed his eyes. "I know and I appreciate it, but I won't be alone that long and I have my crutches. I'll be fine. I promise."

"All right."

Ric's niece, Hayley, ran into the living room and hopped up on the couch beside him. She wrapped her arms around his neck and gave him a noisy kiss on the cheek while Coco jumped onto the couch and tried to squirm in between them.

"You have a good day," she said, her blue eyes smiling.

Ric kissed her nose. "I will. Go learn lots, okay?"

"Okay." She wiggled down off the couch and Coco yipped and ran after her.

Ric looked back up at Emily. "Go take your girl to school. Me and the dog will be fine."

"Well, after what happened the other day, I've decided to take Coco along when I take Hayley to school," Emily said. "I won't be long."

"Go!"

"Okay, okay!"

Ric blew out a sigh of relief when she left the room. He ran a hand through his hair and tried to let his frustration go. He picked up the remote and turned on the TV as he heard Emily and Hayley leave.

He flipped through several channels and then looked at his left ankle in dismay. He'd come to Cooper's Creek for Hayley's eighth birthday party a week and a half ago and he'd slipped on black ice when he'd been getting out of his rental car at the grocery store in town. Although they were heading into spring, the nights were cold.

He'd gone down heavily and his foot had gotten caught in the door somehow, fracturing two of the bones in his ankle. Emily had been up his ass ever since he'd come home from the ER. While he was grateful to her and her husband, Tyler, for letting him stay with them while he recovered, he could see that Emily was going to test his patience with her constant mothering.

After clicking through a bunch of shows and infomercials that didn't hold his interest, he turned on Sports Center. Nothing on there, either. Of course, it was only seven-thirty a.m., so there wasn't going to be much on TV at that time of day. Normally, he'd already be at work. He ran the New York division of Horizon Enterprises, a highly successful investment firm.

Tyler, who was one of his best friends, now ran the Denver office, and their other best friend, Chase McIntyre, ran their L.A. office. With a smile as he thought about Chase, Ric picked up his phone and hit the Skype icon. It would only be 5:30 a.m. there and rousting Chase's annoying ass from bed would be fun.

Chase answered but he wasn't in the frame anywhere.

"Hang on!" Ric heard him say, followed by heavy breathing. "Oh, God. Can't stop. Gotta keep going!"

"Jesus, Chase! Why do you answer when you're in the middle of sex?" Ric asked, about to hang up.

"I'm not! I'm running, but I'm almost done. Hang on!"

Ric leaned his head back against the couch while he waited.

"Okay."

Ric saw a very sweaty Chase smiling at him. "Why are you up so early?"

"I ain't been to bed yet. Couldn't sleep, so I decided to take a run on the beach while the sun came up. Look at that." Chase turned the phone around so that Ric could see the beautiful sunrise over the beach. "Isn't that gorgeous?"

"Yeah, it is. How come you couldn't sleep?"

"Too jazzed up from a late-night Creative session."

"Are you sure that's all it was?" Ric's brotherly-like concern rose.

"Positive. It was a great session, too. I sent you and Ty the preliminary stuff we came up with, but you're supposed to be relaxing. And you shouldn't look at business stuff if you're on pain killers. You'll screw something up. How are you feeling?"

Ric shifted his ankle a little. "Been better, been worse.

I'll live."

"Glad to hear it."

"I'm bored."

Chase laughed. "I knew you would be. Come to Creative Day later. Noon your time. If nothing else, you'll have fun. Especially if you pop a couple of pills beforehand."

Ric grinned at the idea of attending Creative Day via Skype while hopped up on hydrocodone. "I just might do that, if for no other reason than to keep Emily from smothering me."

"Aw, don't be hard on your baby sis. She's just worried about you," Chase said. "I wish my sisters gave a shit about me."

Ric felt a pang of sympathy as he watched Chase's smile disappear. "Sorry, buddy."

The smile returned. "No, worries. Well, I'm gonna go home and see if Sweet Shelly is still in my bed. That's the lovely lady I saw a few times this week. If so, I'll work off some more energy and maybe get a nap in. See ya at Creative Day."

"Wait, wait! Who is this girl? Anyone serious?"

Chase laughed. "Naw. Neither of us is looking for something serious."

"How come you're not looking for serious? You have such a big heart."

That was Chase to a T. Everyone loved Chase and he loved just about everyone, even people he didn't agree with. He was a proud tree hugger and did whatever he could to limit his carbon footprint, which included biking or walking almost everywhere and recycling everything that could be.

He also used mass transportation and hated Ric's Hummer with a passion because of how much gas it guzzled.

The little garden that Chase had planted on the Rooftop, which was what he called the roof of their L.A. headquarters, was used to grow organic vegetables. Chase loved working up there with his adorable dog, Lola, and so did the employees. Chase's office had the lowest staff turnover across the group. The Rooftop had been made into an informal boardroom that was designed to promote creativity and positive energy.

Some days the work done there was very focused, while other days Chase had food and drinks served. They also played games that tended to generate ideas and relieve stress. It was vastly different than the way Ric and Tyler ran their operations, but then Chase's role in their company was marketing, not investment strategy.

"Some men are just not the serious kind," Chase replied. "I'm one of them. You on the other hand... How come you're not looking for serious? You're just as much of a playboy as I am but I don't think you're happy."

Ric said, "So many women and not enough time. Isn't that our motto?"

"For me, perhaps. Listen, sorry but I gotta scoot. Check ya later," Chase said. "Chase, out!"

As he hung up, Ric thought about Chase's comments. Was he happy? New York and his job were very satisfying but he'd been restless of late.

Chase was a brilliant marketer, and hid a wicked intellect behind his playboy, happy-go-lucky persona. But Ric sensed Chase's insecurities. Chase's relationship with his father was toxic and Ric remembered the unhappy boy who'd arrived in

Coopers Creek after his parent's divorce.

Ric made a mental note to have a serious chat with his friend when they next met face to face, then Ric decided to take a look at the stuff that Chase had sent him. He grabbed his laptop from the coffee table and had just opened it when Emily and Coco returned. The chocolate bundle of energy bounded up onto the couch and wiggled her whole body in happiness to see Ric.

The puppy was cute as hell, all paws and wicked tail. Her amber eyes shone at Ric from beneath brown eyebrows as she plopped a red ball down next to Ric.

Ric knew that if he started playing fetch with Coco, she'd play until she dropped. "Not right now, girl. I have work to do."

Coco nudged the ball against Ric's leg.

Emily came into the living room. "You can babysit her while I work."

Ric gave her an irritated look. "I have work to do, too. I have to look over these ads and reports Chase sent me and I have to go to Creative Day later."

Emily pursed her lips. "Well, at least keep her occupied while I make you something to eat, then you can take your pain meds. You're not supposed to take them on an empty stomach."

Ric groaned. "Yes, Mother."

Emily flipped him off and left the room. Ric sighed as he picked up Coco's ball and threw it. He hoped that he healed quickly so he could get back to New York as soon as possible.

*****

Two days later, Ric was going out of his mind from all of

his forced inactivity. The amount of work he could do was limited and his ankle was painful, which made him cranky. Once again, Emily had made him comfortable in the living room since she had to take Coco to the vet for a checkup.

"Emily, I need to get out of the house for a while. I know it's last minute, but I'm going to go along for the ride," he said.

The image of Kate rose in his mind, just as it had several times a day ever since he'd met her. Not only would the ride be good for him, but he'd also have a chance to thank her for cleaning up after Coco that day.

"Oh, okay. I'll get your coat."

Ric stood up and grabbed his crutches. He swung out to the kitchen, ignoring the throbbing in his ankle as best he could and balanced on his good leg to put on his coat. Emily put Coco's leash on her and they went out to Emily's Subaru. Ric carefully got in and it wasn't long before they were underway.

After being stuck in the house, it felt like heaven to have a change of scenery, even if the April sky was overcast and rain had been forecasted. Coco pressed her nose against the rear window on his side. Ric got a kick out of the way she barked at blowing leaves, people, or just about anything that moved. One of the neighbors on their road hadn't taken down a giant Santa Claus and the sight of it sent Coco into hysterics.

"I don't know why she hates that thing so much," Emily said. "She does that every time we go past it."

Ric pet Coco to soothe her. "What's the matter, honey? Are you mad at Santa because he didn't bring you what you wanted for Christmas?"

Coco gave an affirmative woof, which made them laugh.

"So how's Mommy feeling today?" Ric asked.

Emily was four months along now, and just really beginning to show. She beamed with happiness. "Mommy is feeling just fine."

"I'm really happy for you and Ty," Ric said. "I'm glad he stopped being an asshole and that things worked out for you."

Emily nodded. "Me, too. We worked through a lot of things. Nothing is completely one-sided. I made mistakes, too. I won't pretend I didn't. But that's all in the past and we're so excited about this baby and about having primary custody of Hayley."

Ric quickly squashed a momentary flash of jealousy. He had to get over that. He'd been in love with Hayley's mother, Lizzie, who'd died in a car accident. Hayley had been left parentless since her father, Simon, had run off. Ric might have been in love with Lizzie, a reckless, wild child, but she'd let him think there was more and then slipped away. She'd been too young and too wild to understand the depth of what he'd felt for her. He was slowly coming to grips with that and trying to forgive her.

Ric had still been crushed by her death because he'd never stopped loving her. He'd held out hope that she would've come to her senses and ditched Simon for him. He would've taken care of her and Hayley. It was those feelings that had fostered the deep attachment he felt to Hayley. Ric tried not to overstep his bounds where Hayley was concerned, but he couldn't help spoiling her.

"I can't believe how reasonable Simon has been about the whole situation," Ric said. "It took a lot of balls to come back, I'll give him that."

Emily slowed down as they entered the town limits. "Yeah. He's really turned his life around. I have to give him credit. Ty still hates him, but he's trying to be civil for Hayley's sake."

Ric was also trying to forgive Simon. Jealousy and anger at what happened to Lizzie still made him want to smash Simon's smug face every now and then. "Tyler can be hardheaded, and that's an understatement," Ric said. "But he's got Hayley's best interests at heart, so he'll do the right thing." *Listen to yourself for a change. You need to be civil to Simon too.*

She turned right at the town square. "Yeah. Under that sometimes tough exterior of his, he's a big softie."

They arrived at the vet's office and Ric waited until Emily exited the car with Coco before he got out. He followed Emily inside and took a seat in the waiting area while Emily checked in.

A woman in scrubs came around the corner of a hallway that led to exam rooms and Ric's blood pressure rose as he recognized Kate. Her mahogany hair was pulled up a ponytail, which showed off her high cheekbones and luminous dark eyes. She looked almost as fantastic in scrubs as she did in jeans.

Damn, she is one fine-looking woman. I wouldn't mind if she examined me. He couldn't keep his eyes off her and when her gaze met his, he didn't look away. Ric was the kind of man that went after something when he wanted it, and he wanted Kate. He pushed all his doubts away.

She smiled and gave him a little wave. Ric raised an eyebrow and motioned her over.

"Hi, Doc. How are you?" he asked when she stood before him.

"I'm good, thanks. How's the ankle?"

"I'll live. Thanks for everything the other day. You didn't have to do that," Ric said.

Kate tucked an errant lock of hair behind her ear and he wanted to suck on her pretty earlobe. "I was happy to do it. You weren't in any shape to clean up and I didn't feel right leaving things that way."

"I really appreciate it. In fact, I'd like to take you to dinner to repay you."

Her eyebrows drew together as her expression turned uncertain. "I don't know. My schedule is pretty hectic."

Ric wasn't going to give up. "Well, mine is pretty flexible since I can't work a whole lot. So, whenever is good for you works for me."

"I can't."

The sudden sadness in her eyes piqued Ric's curiosity. "Are you involved with someone? I'm sorry. I didn't think about that."

Kate shook her head. "No, I'm not seeing anyone. I'm not looking for anyone, either."

"Oh, I see. Look, this would be just a simple thank you dinner. Or how about I buy you lunch, if that makes you more comfortable? Tomorrow at the Diner?"

Her inner struggle clearly showed on her face. Then she nodded. "All right. Lunch it is. Around one, as long as something doesn't come up."

Ric smiled, surprised at how happy her acceptance of his invitation made him. "Great. I'm looking forward to it."

She gave him a small smile. "Me, too. Well, I'd better

take a look at Coco. I'll see you tomorrow."

"Tomorrow," Ric agreed.

Kate smiled again before turning around and greeting Emily. "Come on back with me," she said.

Emily sent a grin over her shoulder to Ric as she followed Kate back to an exam room with Coco. Ric smiled back and shrugged a shoulder. He didn't feel bashful about asking Kate out. There was just something about the woman that drew him like a magnet to metal, and he intended to see if the feeling was mutual or if he was tilting at windmills.

Chapter Three

Throughout the rest of Kate's day, thoughts of Ric distracted her from her work. It wasn't like her to be so unfocused, but she couldn't help it. Why had she agreed to meet him for lunch? She hadn't had any interest in men since her fiancé, Phil, had passed away. A piece of her heart had shriveled and died with him.

His death had left her with a bleeding, gaping wound that would never be healed. Her job had been her salvation. She'd thrown herself into her business to keep from going insane from grief. If she'd allowed herself to wallow, Kate knew that she might've done something desperate.

She'd been approached by a few men, but she'd nicely rebuffed them. What made Ric different? As she went about stitching and bandaging wounds and giving advice on flea control, a part of her mind was on the incredibly handsome man with the intense blue eyes and a devastating smile.

Towards the end of the day, she grew frustrated with

herself. *It's just lunch. There's no need to panic over lunch! Stop being such a dumbass about this.* It was nothing more than a casual meal. With that decided, Kate was able to stop obsessing and finish out her day with a clearer mind.

*****

As he rode in Emily's car the next day, Ric berated himself for asking Kate to lunch. Not because he didn't want to see her, but because he had to be driven to the Diner like a kid who wasn't old enough to drive. Being laid up was seriously interfering with his independence and it made him short-tempered.

Looking over at Emily, he felt contrite. "Em, I'm sorry that I've been such an ass the last few days. I'm just not used to depending on people to take care of me."

She gave him a wry smile. "Apology accepted and I'm sorry for acting like you're a child. It's just that you took such good care of me after Mom died that I wanted to return the favor."

Now Ric felt like an even bigger dick. "That's what big brothers are supposed to do."

"But not all big brothers would," Emily said.

"Yeah, well, that's because they're selfish assholes."

Emily laughed as she turned at the square. "True. But you have one of the biggest hearts around and I'm very grateful. How about this? I won't smother you and you let people help you when you need it. Deal?"

"I can live with that. Deal."

Flurries started drifting down from the sky as Emily pulled up in front of the Diner.

"Are you going to be all right? Do you need help getting out?" she asked.

Ric leaned over and kissed her cheek. "Nope. I got this. I'll call you when I'm done. Thanks for everything, sis."

He carefully got out of the car, hopped up onto the sidewalk, and shut her car door. After waving to her, he made his way into the Diner.

"Well, here comes Hop-A-Long!"

Ric grinned as he recognized Tucker McGee's gravelly voice and saw him wave to him from a back booth. "Tucker, you old grease monkey!" he shot back. He looked around, but Kate wasn't there yet.

Tucker laughed and motioned him over to his booth. Ric greeted some other people he knew as he made his way through the place. Once a football hero in a small town, always a football hero.

As he slid into the booth, Ric leaned his crutches against the wall behind him and held out a hand to the fifty-something man. "Good to see you, Tucker."

"Likewise, Ricky," Tucker replied, giving his hand a hearty shake. "Stopped in for a bite to eat, huh?"

"Well, I'm meeting someone here."

Ric looked around at the restaurant that had been simply named the Diner when it had been built in the 1970's. It had been renovated a couple of times, but the retro design of the place had been kept intact. Pictures of important residents of Cooper's Creek hung on many of the walls and the football team was included in that.

Ric knew that he was in a bunch of them and in some pictures of the local rodeo champions, which also included him. He'd earned quite a few roping trophies over the years. He'd actually been considering coming home for the rodeo that year, but he wasn't sure that was going to happen since he'd gotten hurt.

"Meeting someone, huh? What little filly have you roped now?" Tucker's brown eyes gleamed.

"I didn't say it was a woman."

Tucker chuckled as he took a sip of coffee. "No, but a man doesn't say they're meeting someone and then grin like an idiot unless it's a woman. Unless they're gay, but as far as I know, you don't swing that way."

"No, I don't," Ric said. "Speaking of that, how's Sarah?"

A frown passed over Tucker's face in response to Ric's inquiry about his niece. "So-so, I guess. She's trying to move on after that bitch, Roxie, broke her heart. I don't normally believe in hitting women, but in Roxie's case, well, I'd be sorely tempted."

Ric nodded. "I completely understand."

Tucker regarded him seriously. "I'm glad you and Ty patched things up. You've been friends for too long not to. It takes a big man to admit that he's wrong and apologize for it."

"It was hard for a while. Emily's my baby sister and no one screws with her, you know? Not even my best friend."

"I hear ya. But you seem like it worked out the way it was supposed to," Tucker commented.

"Yeah." Ric looked at his watch. Kate was almost fifteen minutes late and he had the sinking feeling that she wasn't going to make it.

"Uh oh. Your filly late?"

Ric nodded. "Yeah. She most likely got held up."

"Who is it?"

Along with being the best mechanic in Cooper's Creek, Tucker was one of the nosiest people Ric knew. Still, there was no point in keeping the identity of his date a secret because he knew that it would be all over town anyway. There were times when Ric found the anonymity of New York a huge relief. You could go days without seeing anyone you knew if you didn't want to. Not so in Cooper's Creek.

"Kate Donoghue."

Tucker leaned over the table conspiratorially. "The sexy vet?" He let out a low whistle. "Holy smokes. She must really like you."

Ric frowned in confusion. "What do you mean?"

"Word around town is that she doesn't date." Tucker finished his coffee and stood up. "Well, I gotta get back to the shop. Hope she doesn't have to cancel on you. Good seeing you. Don't be a stranger, Ricky."

Ric promised not to be and Tucker sauntered away. Taking out his phone, Ric contemplated calling the vet clinic since he hadn't gotten Kate's number from her the other day. He could text Emily for it, but he didn't want her to know that Kate was late. Or maybe she wasn't going to show up at all.

Her hesitancy hadn't been lost on him and he wondered if he'd come on too strong. Sitting his phone on the table, Ric decided to give her a little more time.

*****

Her truck radio blared Miranda Lambert as Kate sat paralyzed behind the steering wheel. Parked just up the street from the Diner, she couldn't make herself shut off the ignition and go meet Ric. It was just lunch, but suddenly it seemed like more than that.

And, in a way it was, because it would be the first time

since Phil had died that she'd be sitting down to a meal with a single man. What did that signify? Was she ready to move on? Judging by the way she was trembling, it didn't feel like it.

Why did I agree to this? Stupid! Anger surfaced as she berated herself for being scared.

"It's just lunch! Get the hell in there!"

She wrenched the ignition off, grabbed her purse, and got out of her blue F150. Decisively, she shut and locked the door. Kate threw her keys in her purse and walked swiftly towards the restaurant. Going inside, she looked around, but she didn't see Ric at first. Then she spotted an arm waving and her gaze collided with his.

All of the oxygen seemed to have been sucked out of the place, making it hard to breathe. His dimpled smile and piercing blue eyes almost turned her into a puddle right on the spot. She waved back and gave him what she was sure was a goofy smile before forcing herself to start towards him. Her heart throbbed painfully under her ribcage as she neared him.

He looked like a cross between a sexy lumberjack and a walking advertisement for L.L. Bean. The blue-and-black checkered flannel shirt he wore emphasized his broad shoulders and brought out the color of his eyes even more. His blond hair was attractively tousled in a way that made her want to run her fingers through it.

"Hi. Pardon me for not standing."

His deep voice washed over her like a warm ocean tide and Kate wanted to get pulled into the undertow.

Kate smiled at his joke and sat down. "I'll forgive you this time."

"Thanks. How are you?"

The way he said it told Kate that he was genuinely interested. "I'm good, thanks. Busy. It's been busy. I guess that's good, though. Job security." Suddenly, she felt panicky and wanted to flee.

She jumped a little when Ric put his hand over hers where it rested on the table and rubbed his thumb over her knuckles.

"Kate, we're just having lunch, that's all. Nothing more, okay?"

Kate looked at his hand, which was so much larger than her own. His powers of perception were amazing. Ric's touch was gentle, hypnotizing, and she felt calm enough now to laugh a little. "I'm sorry. I'm being silly. It's just that I haven't been out with anyone in a long time." She bit her bottom lip in trepidation. "Not since my fiancé passed away."

Ric's eyebrows went up and then a look of sympathy crossed his face. "I'm so sorry. I had no idea."

He withdrew his hand and she wished he hadn't. "It's okay. It was eighteen months ago."

"I lost a woman I loved eight years ago and it still hurts sometimes. I know how you feel, but I'm sure it has to be worse for you," Ric said.

"How so?"

His mouth curved a little in a sad smile. "She didn't love me back."

Kate's heart hurt for him. At least she knew that Phil had loved her. Unrequited love was a terrible thing to endure. "Well, I don't really know you, but something tells me that she was a fool."

"Thanks." His smile reached his eyes this time. "I'm glad we got all of that out of the way."

Kate was surprised how relieved and lighter she felt. "Me, too." Why had she felt so comfortable in confiding in him so quickly? She decided not to examine it.

Ric shifted a little. "Kate, you need to know that I'm not looking for anything serious. I'm going back to New York as soon as my ankle is healed enough. I head up the Horizon Enterprises division there. But you're a beautiful, kind, intelligent woman and I'd like to get to know you better." He sent her a charming, confident smile. "I think we could have some fun before I leave, perhaps we could both do with some fun?

Fun. Kate couldn't remember the last time she'd had any real fun. She gone out a few times with her best friend, Robert, to a couple of bars, but that was only because he'd kept pestering her. Besides, she had heard all about Ric's reputation with the ladies. The High School Jock had been quite the heart breaker and from what she knew of his life in New York that had not changed.

But Kate reminded herself she wasn't looking to give her heart to anyone any time soon. Her body... now where would be the harm in that.

Looking at Ric, whose eyes held a wicked gleam, Kate could well imagine what sort of fun he was talking about. Heat suffused her body and the Diner suddenly seemed overly warm. Her stomach tightened with a sensation she hadn't felt in so long. Desire. Pure, hot, desire.

Recklessly, Kate said, "I could stand to have some fun. I don't want anything serious, either."

His smile broadened. "Perfect. Nothing heavy, nothing

but two people enjoying time together."

It certainly sounded perfect and Kate wondered again what was so different about Ric that she'd agreed to something like that so eagerly? That impulsive voice in her brain told her reasonable side to shut the hell up and Kate listened to it.

"Exactly. Now, what are you going to have to eat? I'm starving and I have a full afternoon," she said.

Ric picked up his menu, looked at it for two seconds, put it down, and gave her a cheeky grin. "I knew what I wanted before I came in here."

Kate couldn't resist his playful behavior. "I'll just bet you did. I'm afraid to ask."

He quirked an eyebrow. "You naughty girl, Dr. Donoghue. I'm not sure what you're referring to, but I was talking about an open-faced roast beef sandwich with gravy fries and apple pie."

"Well, well, Mr. Stanford, you even know what you want for dessert already."

"I never kid around about dessert. That's serious business." He picked up his menu and pretended that it was a sheaf of papers, which he straightened. "Now, I picked the apple pie because it's very American, which is very important when you're trying to convince an American veterinarian to engage in an enjoyable lunch with you."

Kate folded her arms. "What if I was British?"

"I'd still choose American because the British secretly love Americans. Canadians, however, hate us," Ric said.

"Canadians hate us?"

Ric nodded. "With a passion. I know a guy who used to work at a call center for a heating company that had a bunch of franchises in Canada. If the Canadians figured out that he was American when they called to set up service calls, he got ripped a new one. Most of the time, the customers demanded to talk to whatever Canadian supervisor was around."

Kate laughed. "What did he do?"

Ric grinned. "What could he do? He put the customer on hold and came back after a minute and pretended to be Canadian."

"How do you pretend to be Canadian?"

"Well, there are certain words that they pronounce differently than us and they don't say the letter 'z' like us. They say 'zed'. X,Y, Zed. Stuff like that."

"So he faked being a Canadian supervisor so that he didn't get yelled at by Canadians?"

"Mmm hmm. Which is hard to do with a Texan accent. But my friend is resourceful like that," Ric told her.

"He sounds funny."

"He is, but back to this pie situation. What kind are you going to have?"

"We haven't even gotten to order lunch yet," Kate said.

Ric held up a hand and waved. "Cletus! Where's Portia? We're starving over here!"

Kate's face turned pink as she giggled, but Ric's confident, authoritative manner wasn't lost on her. Obviously, he was the sort of man who was used to being obeyed when he gave an order.

"Portia! Go get Ricky's order!" hollered a man from the kitchen.

"Ricky, huh?" Kate teased.

Ric made a face. "Cletus has known me since I was born. Portia and I went to high school together." He sighed. "I'll

30

always be Ricky to some of the people around here."

"Your sister doesn't call you that."

"Nope. Took a while to break her, though," Ric said as a slim blonde sashayed up to their table.

"Hi, Ricky. Sorry to keep you waiting." She pointedly ignored Kate as she smiled ingratiatingly at Ric. "How's your ankle?"

Kate was startled to see Ric's whole demeanor change. One minute, he'd been warm and amusing and the next cold and businesslike.

"Fine, thanks. We'd like to order, please."

Portia pouted at his abrupt statement. "Fine. What'll you have?"

They placed their order and Portia left, but the angry glint in Ric's eyes didn't completely fade.

"Is there something wrong?" Kate asked.

Ric shook his head. "No. I just have to put a stop to Portia's behavior before she makes things awkward. She's always had a thing for me, but I've never been attracted to her. I'd rather not give her any hope than respond to her flirting. She doesn't know when to quit so I have to make sure she doesn't even start."

Kate said, "Remind me not to piss you off. You're a little scary."

Ric laughed. "I'm sorry. I don't mean to be. Well, sometimes I do, but not with sexy veterinarians who clean up after puppies when people are too wacked out on pain meds to do it."

And with his witty remark, the previous playful mood was restored and the next half-hour went by before Kate knew it. Ric was so engaging and genuine that she hadn't been paying attention to the time until her text message alert went off.

"Sorry," she said as she hit the message icon. Alarm shot through her when she read the text from Robert. "Oh, God! I'm ten minutes late for an appointment! I have to go. I forgot to set my alarm." She hastily grabbed her coat and stood up. "I had a great time. Thanks so much."

Ric nodded. "Me, too. Is it okay if I call you?"

"Yes. Absolutely." Kate was so rattled that she bent down and kissed Ric's cheek. "Oh, God! I'm sorry. I shouldn't have... I mean, um, I'll see you later."

Kate knew her face was beet red with embarrassment because it felt like it was on fire. She turned and fled the Diner before she did something to make herself look like an even bigger idiot. All the way to her truck, she mentally kicked her ass and when she climbed in the cab, she rested her forehead on the steering wheel and groaned at her stupidity.

Then she started the truck and peeled away, flooring it as she hurried off to the clinic, certain that she'd seen the last of Ric.

Chapter Four

That night, Ric paid for having his ankle down so much during the day, but his lunch with Kate had been worth it. Especially the part at the end where she'd gotten flustered and kissed him. She'd been adorable and hot at the same time and he'd been amused as hell by her.

As he laid awake in what had been Tyler's room when they'd been in high school, playing games on his tablet, Ric contemplated how he was going to go about seeing her again. It was hard when he was laid up. Dancing was out, so was going for romantic moonlight walks or—he jumped when his Skype notification went off loudly in his ear.

He'd put in his earbuds so he could still hear the game without waking anyone up, and so he didn't have to hear anything down the hall he didn't want to. Stifling a laugh when he saw Chase's goofy profile pic, he hit the answer button.

"What are you doing?" he asked.

"I'm on the trampoline. Wanna jump with me?" Chase

asked.

Ric grinned. "Why are you on the trampoline at ten-thirty at night? Why aren't you at a club or something?"

The view of the city in back of Chase rose and fell as Chase bounced on the apparatus. "I have a lovely lady friend stoppin' by later, but for now I'm bouncing like Tigger. Hoo hoo!"

It was a good thing his door was shut because Ric couldn't contain his laughter over Chase's antics. "You're such a fucking dork."

Chase laughed. "I'm just getting ready to bounce *her*, that's all. So, I heard through the grapevine that you had a lunch date today."

"Let me guess; Emily told you."

"Bingo! How'd that go?"

Ric recounted the events of that afternoon.

"You gonna see her again?" Chase asked. "Last jump. Watch this."

Chase executed a flip and Ric felt like he was right there with him as he watched the world spin. He'd jumped on Chase's trampoline and it was fun as hell doing it while watching the L.A. skyline.

The world righted and Chase came back into sight. "Okay. Answer me now."

"I'm definitely going to see her again. She'll have to pick me up, though. I'm not going to have Emily keep driving me everywhere," Ric said.

"Yeah. I can understand that. Pretty embarrassing when you call her to come get you after a spending the night at Kate's house," Chase said. "She can drop you off before she goes to work."

Ric laughed. "Thanks for helping me figure that out. I never thought of that."

"Of course, then you'll have Emily wondering where you are. Better turn your phone off. Don't want it ringing at that special moment. Major buzz kill."

"Tell me about it. I'll give her strict instructions not to call me unless it involves life and limb," Ric said.

"Good idea. You gonna take her to dinner?"

"Yeah, I guess." An idea occurred to Ric. "Actually, no. I have a better idea."

"Lay it on me, big man."

"Nah. I'm going to keep you in suspense. Plus, I'd rather wait until after the fact in case it winds up being a clusterfuck."

Chase nodded. "Okay. Whatever helps you sleep at night."

"Hey, speaking of sleeping at night, how come you're not? And don't feed me a line of bullshit about Creative sessions, either."

A sigh escaped Chase as he flopped down in a chair. "Brenda called me last week and it stirred up my bees' nest of a past. She's getting out of prison next month and wanted to know if I'd hire her. I said to do what? Rob me blind? I don't think so. Then she tried to get me to loan her money. I turned her down flat. I can't go down that road again, Ric."

After the hell that Chase's sister—and practically his whole family—had put him through, Ric didn't blame his buddy. "Good. I'm glad you didn't let her talk you into it."

"Hell, no. But you know how it twists my guts. She's family," Chase said.

"Sorry. I really don't know what to say that I haven't

said before, but you've given her so many chances already." Ric put a hand over his eyes. "I like that we have each other's backs."

Chase cracked up. "Me to. You mean well. Okay, I gotta go shower and get ready for Her Hotness."

"Shelly?"

"Naw. Shelly got pissed when I asked if Danielle could join us," Chase replied. "So, it's a new lovely lady."

"So you essentially gave Shelly the heave-ho by using your fictitious friend again?"

"Better that they hate me when it's time to say goodbye. Shelly's a great girl, but I think she was measuring my windows for curtains, if you know what I mean," Chase said.

"What are you going to do when you find a woman who says yes when you suggest Danielle coming over?" Ric asked.

Chase's laugh was infectious. "That's the girl I'll marry." He winked and hit the end button.

Ric laughed as he went back to playing his game and figured out the logistics of his plan.

*****

Kate clicked her way around an accounting spreadsheet, playing with numbers to see where her profits were going to end up for the month of April. Business was good, especially because her staff was following her instructions to push flea control products and healthy pet treats.

When her phone rang, she picked it up and hit the answer button without looking to see who it was. "Hello, Doc. How's the sexiest veterinarian I know?"

Kate almost dropped the phone in surprise as she recognized his voice. "Ric?"

"Yeah. How are you?"

"I'm, uh, fine, and you?" Kate cursed herself for tripping all over her tongue, but she was shocked to hear from him.

"I'm good. I was wondering if you were free for dinner tonight?"

His voice was a cross between sandpaper and satin and it stirred her nerve endings. If he affected her this way by just talking to her, she could only imagine what it would be like to kiss him, or—

"Kate? You there?"

"Yeah. I'm just surprised to hear from you after the other day," she said.

"You mean because you kissed me?"

A blush spread over her cheeks even though she couldn't see him. "Yes."

Ric's laugh was warm and inviting. "Are you kidding me? I loved it. There's no reason to be embarrassed."

"I just want you to know that I don't go around kissing men I just met, okay?"

"So it's just me, huh?"

Kate put a hand to her forehead as she laughed. "Yes. I haven't done that in so long."

His voice deepened a note. "I'm glad it's me, and if you agree to dinner with me, there'll be a lot more kissing involved."

Right then, Kate wished he was right there with her because she wanted him to kiss her. *What's the matter with me? I'm acting like a horny teenager!* "I'll agree to dinner, but I'm not sure about the other part."

"I can live with that. What time is good for you?"

"I'm leaving in about an hour."

"I'll meet you at the clinic," Ric said.

Kate sat up straighter. "Oh, well, I'd like to go home and clean up so I don't smell like animals."

Ric chuckled. "Don't worry, where we're going, it won't matter. I'll see you at six. Bye, Doc."

He hung up before she could object and Kate stared at the phone for a moment. Where were they going? She didn't want to meet him wearing scrubs and Crocs.

"Jeans! I have jeans in the truck!" Kate stood up so fast that she banged her knee on her desk. "Shit!"

She always kept a change of clothes in her truck because she never knew what she'd come up against when she got called out to a farm. That way, she was always prepared. It was her saving grace right then.

Hurrying out the back door, she ran to her truck and retrieved the duffle bag behind the driver's seat. Back inside, she ran into Robert Chambers, her office manager and best friend.

"There you are. I wanted to talk to you about one of our purchase orders," he said.

"Oh, uh, sure," she said. "Just be quick about it because I have a few things to do before I leave at six."

Robert nodded. "Okay."

He followed Kate into her office and they went over an order for surgical supplies that needed to be changed. Kate kept glancing at the clock on the wall.

"Am I keeping you from something?" Robert asked.

Kate gave him an apologetic smile. "Well, sort of. I'm meeting someone after work and I need to change."

Robert lifted a dark eyebrow. "Oh, I see. Who is he?"

"I'd rather not say. We just had lunch together. There's

not much to tell," Kate said.

"This is a big step for you. Are you sure you're ready?" Robert asked.

Kate nodded. "Neither one of us want anything serious. Just some companionship and fun. We're keeping it light."

Concern shone in Robert's brown eyes. "I think that's a good idea. I'm not trying to be a killjoy. God knows you deserve some fun, but I just don't want you to jump too far, too fast."

"You're absolutely right," Kate agreed. "I don't have the time or the heart for anything serious. I'm not ready for that. Someday, but not now." She smiled. "But in the meantime, I think some fun is just what the doctor ordered."

Robert groaned at her bad pun. "You need to brush up on your witty banter, Kate."

"Get out of here." She shoved him playfully. "I have to get ready."

"At least tell me what he looks like," Robert said.

"Blond hair, blue eyes, and a body to die for."

"Like Brad Pitt?"

Kate laughed. "He makes Brad Pitt look like an ugly duckling."

Robert's eyes widened. "Holy shit. That hot, huh?"

"Yes. Now go!" Kate said.

Although she could tell that Robert wanted to ask more questions, he reluctantly left her office. Kate locked the door and quickly got rid of her scrubs. Yanking open her bottom desk drawer, she found deodorant, a small vial of perfume and a couple of pairs of earrings.

She was glad to see that the jeans in her duffel bag weren't too wrinkled as she shimmied into them. Then she yanked the lavender cable-knit sweater over her head and settled it into place. Looking in the mirror on the back of her office door, Kate saw that her hair was full of static and stuck up here and there.

Grabbing her purse, she pulled out her brush and quickly put her long tresses in a single braid. She put on a little pink lipstick and some mascara and was finished with three minutes to spare.

"That's as good as it gets," she muttered. "Not bad. He'll have to be happy with that on such short notice."

Then she laughed at her grumpy remark, shoved her scrubs into her duffel bag, and tidied up her office again. With a last look in the mirror, she took a deep breath and left the office. She said goodnight to her staff and stepped outside to see Ric leaning against a tree close to the clinic.

The way he looked in his navy blue sweatpants and heavy denim coat gave her a fluttery sensation in her stomach. His choice in pants made sense since they would go up over his cast easily. No man had ever made sweatpants look so hot. Now she knew why he hadn't cared about her getting all dressed up.

He saw her and pushed off the tree. Ric started for her and Kate wondered how he made moving on crutches look sexy. As he neared her, the predatory gleam in his eyes made the flutter in her stomach change to the kind of ache she'd almost forgotten had existed.

Ric didn't stop until he'd slightly invaded her personal space. "Hi, Kate."

Suddenly, she felt like she was sixteen again and had a huge crush on the high school quarterback, who'd actually stopped to speak to her. His bulk and the incredible way he smelled rendered her speechless for a few moments. "Hi, Ric," she finally said, hating that she sounded a little breathy.

His gaze slowly traveled over her as though he wanted to devour her and her pulse rose. When he leaned towards her, it never crossed her mind to back away from him. His lips on her cheek were warm and firm and she wanted to feel them on hers.

"I owed you that," he said, smiling as he drew away.

Kate hid the fact that her heart had just flipped over by chuckling. "I still can't believe I did that."

Ric said, "I didn't mind a bit."

"I'm glad," Kate responded. "My truck is right over here. So, where is our mystery designation?"

"The Hamilton Farm."

"The swanky horse farm?" Kate asked as she held open the passenger side of the truck.

Ric handed her his crutches and hopped up in the truck. "Yep. I used to work there back in high school and I'm still friendly with the family."

Kate gave him his crutches and walked around to the driver's side. "You're not going to try to ride with a broken ankle are you?"

Ric grinned. "No. I'm stupid, but not that dumb."

"What are we going to do then?" She started the ignition.

"You'll just have to wait and see."

She met his Cheshire cat smile with a scowl, which made him laugh as she pulled out of the parking lot.

Chapter Five

Ric was getting a kick out of Kate's reaction to his secrecy. They were on Hamilton land now, traveling over a narrow dirt road as the sun was setting. The pinks, purples, and orange hues in the sky provide a romantic backdrop for the mountains in the distance.

He'd loved working for the Hamiltons, especially because they'd let him use their horses whenever he'd wanted to. Emily had always been thrilled when she could go with him to the horse farm to ride. He'd learned to rope on some of the finest Quarter horses in Colorado and had a pile of rodeo trophies in a storage unit out by the highway.

"Are you going to tell me what that smile is about?"

Kate's question drew Ric out of his memories. "I used to spend as much time here as I could when we were kids. Riding, roping, barrel racing: you name it we did it, or tried to anyway. I can ride broncs, but I'm not as good at it as Tyler is. Emily used to be great at barrel racing and a fair roper, too."

"I'd love to see you rope. I love riding, but I've never roped," she said.

Ric said, "I'd be happy to teach you." He could think of a lot of things he'd like to do with her and ropes. "We'd have to start out with easy stuff and work our way up from there."

"Sounds like fun. And I'll teach you to hang-glide in return."

Ric stared at her for a moment. "You hang-glide?"

She nodded and glanced his way. "Oh, yeah. I love it. Rock climbing, cliff diving, and kayaking, too."

He'd obviously misjudged Kate. Apparently, she was a risk-taker and he wasn't sure how he felt about that. "I never would've guessed that about you."

Kate laughed. "I hide my impulsive nature when I'm at work, but I'm a true weekend warrior. I always have been. When other girls were too afraid to go on rollercoasters, I was the first one in line to get on the biggest, baddest coasters. I love amusement parks."

"Me, too," Ric said. "Looks like we have a lot in common."

"Looks like."

Ric had her take the next right and, they soon pulled up in front of a small cabin. Smoke curled from the little chimney and light shone in the windows.

"Who lives here?" she asked.

"No one. All of this land belongs to the Hamiltons. Us kids used to come here to hang out."

"What are we doing here?"

"Stay right there." Ric got out and came around to her

side, where he opened the door. Holding out a hand to her, he said, "We're having dinner."

The curiosity in her eyes made him smile. He knew that she didn't need his help getting out of the truck, but it was the gentlemanly thing to do and it gave him an excuse to touch her.

"I hope you're hungry," he said and motioned for her to precede him into the cabin.

*****

Kate didn't know what to expect when she entered the cabin, but it wasn't what she found. A fire burned in the hearth and two kerosene lamps provided warmth and lighting. She felt like she'd stepped back in time as she looked around at the rustic furnishings. A small table with a red-and-white checkered table cloth covered a small, square table. Three chairs were situated around it.

An old rocking chair sat in one corner, while in another corner, stood a narrow bed with an old fashioned wrought iron bedstead. A beautiful calico red, blue, and gold patchwork quilt covered it and a couple of open-faced cupboards took up the last corner.

Kate turned her gaze on Ric. "This is so charming. I can't believe you did this." It was one of the most romantic things a man had ever done for her.

His warm smile captivated her. "I'm glad you like it. We used to stay here when we were kids and people still use it sometimes. Have a seat." His crutches made it a little awkward, but he pulled out one of the chairs for her.

Kate sat and watched as he sat in another chair. He reached under the table and pulled out a large picnic basket. She'd been looking around at the quaint furnishings too much to have noticed it before.

From the basket he removed a bottle of red wine and two wine glasses and several covered platters. She watched in amazement as he uncovered roasted chicken, Chantilly potatoes, and steamed broccoli. Fresh baked rolls were wrapped up in aluminum foil and he'd also packed condiments.

She laughed with delight. "Well, Mr. Stanford, you certainly go all out when you're trying to impress a woman."

"I don't do anything halfway." He was glad that he'd achieved his objective. "When I'm on a mission, I don't quit until I've succeeded."

The lamplight made her dark eyes even more luminous and Ric could've gazed into them all night.

Kate asked, "Did you cook all of this?"

Ric gave a self-deprecating laugh. "No. Cooking is definitely not my strong suit. Emily is the cook in the family and she was only too happy to help me out."

"Remind me to thank her," Kate said.

"Will do."

Once the meal was assembled and their plates filled, they started eating and it was quiet for a little bit. However, it was an easy, comfortable silence. Ric watched Kate eat, finding it refreshing to see a woman enjoy her food. A lot of his dates were overly delicate about the way they ate.

He knew that it was because they were trying to impress upon him how womanly and desirable they were, but Ric preferred a woman who was genuine and down-to-earth. Most of the time he didn't care all that much because he only had one goal in mind: sex.

His job as CEO of the New York office was demanding,

to say the least, and he didn't have time for romantic entanglements. Therefore, casual, meaningless sex was exactly what he wanted. A way to have some fun and blow off some steam was all he needed.

But as his dinner with Kate proceeded, Ric found himself genuinely interested in her as a person. She was articulate and humorous and he was captivated by her laugh. It had been a long time since Ric had found a woman he wanted to know more about.

He also wanted her intensely and by the time they were ready for the Boston cream pie, Ric was glad that his lap was hidden by the table. Normally, he could keep control of his libido, but there was something about Kate that kicked it into overdrive. He hadn't felt like that since his teenage years. *And Lizzie.*

As they finished the pie, he noticed Kate fidgeting with her fork a little.

"Is everything all right?" he asked.

She licked her lips nervously. "Well, I couldn't help noticing that you brought me somewhere with a bed. What were you expecting to happen tonight?"

Ric leaned back in his chair a little and smiled. "What I was expecting was that we could get to know each other better in a unique, cozy place where we weren't distracted by waiters and other diners. I spend so much of my time in places like that and I was looking forward to doing something different for a change. Plus, call me crazy, but for some reason, I wanted you to see a small piece of my youth. Spending the evening with a beautiful, fun, intelligent woman was all that I was expecting. I swear."

She sent him a flirty little smile that sent his blood

pressure higher. "So you weren't expecting anything to happen on that bed?"

Ric took a sip of wine. "No. Hoping, but not expecting."

She swallowed and Ric wanted to bite her pretty neck. "I see. Ric—"

"I was hoping that I could put my foot up for a little while we watch the fire and talk longer," he said. "I promise that nothing will happen that you don't want to happen, Kate."

*****

His relaxed, self-assured posture told Kate that he was a man who was used to controlling situations, but the honesty in his voice convinced her that he truly was letting her take the lead. What *did* she want to happen? He was so damn good-looking and genuine and nice…How was a woman supposed to resist all of that? Why would she want to?

Phil had been gone for eighteen long, lonely months. Wasn't it time to move on? Kate wanted to move on very badly. She wanted to stop hurting and begin living again. Wouldn't having fun with Ric help her do that? *Damn straight it will!*

Rising, she held out her hand to him. "Come on, cowboy. Let's go talk."

He took her hand and stood up, seeming to tower over her. The light in his eyes reminded her of the way a cougar watches its prey and she was his willing victim. She was surprised when he didn't bother with his crutches and just hopped over to the bed.

The mattress sagged a little as he sat on it. His powerful shoulders bunched under his Broncos sweatshirt as he pulled himself back on the bed until his back rested against the wall.

He patted the spot next to him. "Come on. There's

plenty of room for you."

Kate kicked off her cowboy boots and took off his sneaker. "We don't want to get that pretty quilt dirty."

"Good idea."

The wine made Kate feel reckless and she wanted to shock him. Crawling onto the mattress, she moved across it, right up to him and straddled his hips. His eyes widened for a few moments while she settled into place.

"Hi," she said softly.

"Hi."

She put her hands on his shoulders and met his heated gaze. "We can talk this way, can't we?"

"We certainly can. What would you like to talk about?"

The feel of him between her legs was incredible. She'd forgotten what a heady sensation it was to be seductive, to turn the tables on a man. Leaning forward, Kate laid a hand against Ric's jaw and brushed her lips over his in a teasing kiss that whetted her appetite for more. He smelled incredible, like chocolate with a hint of musk and citrus.

Hunger, raw and potent rose within her and she pressed her mouth against his in a firm kiss. Ric's lips were sensual and warm, inviting her to deepen the kiss. Running the tip of her tongue over his bottom lip, she tasted wine and a hint of their dessert. Suddenly, she was voracious for him and demanded entry.

The growl that rose from his chest as he cupped her head and slanted his mouth over hers sent shivers down her spine. The thrust of his tongue against hers drove away all of her reason. Wrapping her arms around his neck, Kate leaned into him and moaned when she felt his hands settle on the small of her back.

She wanted his hands everywhere, wanted him to kiss her everywhere. Her hips hitched forward of their own accord and Ric must have recognized it for the invitation it was because she felt him undo the button of her jeans and pull the zipper down. She knew that she was moist even before she felt his fingers meet her slick folds.

"Oh, God, yes. Please, Ric."

Opening her eyes, she met his intense gaze as he traced lazy circles around her sensitive nub. The cabin was stifling and she was suffocating in her sweater. She practically ripped it off in her haste to get rid of it. Ric was as carried away as she was and yanked one of her bra cups down as he continued stroking her.

His hot, greedy mouth closed around her nipple and she whimpered in need. Pleasure spiraled inside as he moved faster and suckled hard. Kate couldn't keep still as she shuddered into a blinding climax. She fisted her hands in his sweatshirt and rocked against his hand.

The next moment, the bed gave way and they crashed to the floor.

"Son of a bitch!" Ric shouted as Kate landed hard on top of him.

"Oh, shit! Ric!" Kate scrambled off him and stood up.

"Where the fuck are you going?" he demanded.

Kate was flabbergasted. "We should go. I was going to help you to the truck."

From somewhere underneath him, Ric produced a condom and ripped it open with his teeth. "Like hell you are. Get naked and get the fuck back over here."

His grin as he shoved his sweatpants down made her giggle. The headboard of the bed lay perilously close to his leg. While he gave it a mighty yank and flung it across the room, Kate took the opportunity to appreciate the fact that Ric was very well endowed. His cock proudly stood erect and she quickly shimmied out of her jeans and lacy black underwear.

Ric whipped his sweatshirt over his head and tossed it away before shifting so he could roll the condom down over his length. "Come on, baby. Get over here. We're not done yet."

"Are you sure, Ric? That must've hurt your ankle—"

"Get that sweet ass over here, Kate. I don't give a Goddamn about my ankle right now," Ric said.

Taking him at his word, Kate climbed back onto his lap and straddled him. His gaze never left hers as he guided her slowly down, gradually filling her. Her head fell back on a long sigh as heavenly sensations surged through her.

Ric's large hands skimmed over her hips and up her sides until he cupped her breasts. He teased her nipples with his thumbs and heat pooled where they were joined. Looking down at him, she covered his hands and urged him to squeeze her breasts. She'd missed a man's hands on her body and the way Ric kneaded her firm flesh made her crave more.

*****

Ric loved that Kate was showing him what she liked. He couldn't remember the last time he'd wanted someone so intensely and he was a sucker for a confident, forward woman. Her beautiful breasts and rosy, pink nipples drew his hands and mouth. Playing with them and teasing her with his tongue made him throb.

The more he sucked on her nipples, the more restlessly she moved her hips until she braced her hands on his shoulders and started to rise and fall. Kate had a body built for sex and he wasn't going to let a little thing like a collapsing bed or a broken ankle interfere with enjoying everything she had to offer.

Her smooth, lightly tanned skin was a little flushed and her toned arms and thighs proved that she was a strong, athletic woman. The desire in her deep brown eyes mesmerized him, heightening his own passion.

Ric concentrated on her needs so he could make it last as long as possible for her. "You're so fucking beautiful, Kate. I want you to come for me again. I love how responsive you are."

She smiled at him as her breath quickened. "I couldn't wait. You're so sexy. Too sexy, and you know it."

Ric smiled in acknowledgment before capturing her mouth in a searing kiss. Her lips were so soft and lush and he could imagine how they'd feel on other places of his body. Grasping her hips, he urged her into a faster tempo while using his good leg to thrust upwards.

She clutched his shoulders as she moaned and Ric felt her tight heat clench around his rigid shaft. Sliding his hand down over her stomach to her mound, he stroked her, providing double titillation. His reward was hearing her scream as she threw her arms around his neck and trembled in his arms.

Her pulsing muscles pushed him over the edge and Ric couldn't hold back anymore. He pumped his hips twice before a powerful release rocked through him. Freezing, he pressed his face against her breasts as he groaned in pure ecstasy. It held him for long moments before starting to fade away.

"Oh, shit, Kate," he said, flopping back against the wall. She slid down on top of him. "Oh, shit, is right."

Ric stroked the satiny skin of her back. "Well, that was some very stimulating after dinner conversation."

*****

His chest rumbled with laughter and Kate laughed with him as she thought of the absurdity of the situation.

She leaned back and looked at him. "We broke the bed."

His eyebrows rose. "No, *you* broke the bed with all that rocking you were doing."

Kate put a hand over her mouth. "I couldn't help it. It felt so good and it's been so long."

The enormity of what had just transpired hit Kate with the force of a hammer against glass and her afterglow shattered. She'd just had sex for the first time since Phil had died and she barely knew the guy. And it was her fault. She'd come on to Ric, not the other way around.

Kate's cheeks flamed with embarrassment and regret over her actions, but she didn't want Ric to see her discomfort. She forced a smile as she disentangled herself from him and stood up.

"We better get you home," she said. "Your ankle has to be screaming by now."

Ric sat up as she started gathering her clothing, but Kate studiously avoided his eyes as she stepped into her underwear and pulled on her jeans.

"Kate, what's wrong?"

She sent him a smile that she hoped didn't look as brittle as she felt. "Wrong? Nothing's wrong. It's just getting late and I have a really hectic day tomorrow."

He stood up and Kate couldn't keep her eyes off him any

longer. He'd pulled up his sweatpants, but he was still bare from the waist up. In the heat of the moment, she hadn't taken the time to appreciate his male beauty. His sculpted chest and shoulder muscles bunched and flexed as he hopped over to the table and sat down.

His fine, short golden chest hair caught the lamplight here and there and she thought that he looked more manly than a lot of the guys who waxed their chests these days. He leaned against the chair back and folded his arms over his chest, which drew attention to his huge biceps. Did the man live at the gym? She tried so hard not to compare him to Phil.

"Bullshit, Kate. There's something going on in that beautiful head of yours. If you don't want to talk about it, fine, but don't lie and say that there's nothing wrong."

His directness was refreshing yet annoying. "Okay. I don't care to discuss it."

"Okay."

He calmly shrugged into his sweatshirt and started putting the dirty dishes from supper into the basket as though nothing unusual had just happened. Kate was grateful to him for not pushing because she had so much to process before she talked about what had just happened between them. She should not feel guilty because she'd been with another man. Phil would want her to move on and enjoy her life. But she still missed him and she'd never been one to indulge in meaningless sex. She was scared of what this night meant. She couldn't fall for the playboy.

She helped clean up the cabin and assisted Ric out to the truck before going back in to put out the fire and douse the kerosene lamps. The ride home was largely silent, but Kate had no idea what to say to alleviate the awkwardness.

When they pulled up to the Jeffries house, Kate put the truck in park.

"Ric—"

He put his hand on her forearm. "Don't, Kate." He leaned over and kissed her cheek. "For what it's worth, up until the end, tonight was incredible. I'd like to see you again, but it's your call. I'm also a good listener. Goodnight, Kate."

"Goodnight, Ric."

Tears stood out in her eyes as she waited for him to get safely to the door and go inside. As she turned around and headed back down the driveway, they spilled onto her cheeks and kept falling all the way home.

Chapter Six

"Well, you look like shit."

Kate looked up from her computer to spear Robert with a glare. "Leave me alone."

Robert closed her office door and sat in a chair. "I take it that your date didn't go well."

"I don't want to talk about it."

"But you need to. Get whatever it is off your chest. Not now. We'll go to the Wagon Shed tonight and you can cry into your beer about whatever's bothering you," Robert said.

Kate rubbed her right temple in a poor attempt to alleviate her stress induced headache. She hadn't drunk enough wine the night before to give her a hangover. "I don't know, Robert. After last night, I think I just need a quiet night at home to rest."

Robert made an annoying game show buzzer sound. "Wrong! I'm sorry Dr. Donoghue, but that's not the correct answer! That's the last thing you need. You'll just get stuck up in your head and wallow. No, the right thing to do is to go out, get drunk, and talk it out before it festers. So, I'll pick you up at eight and we'll go do a little commiserating."

Kate eyed him. "What are you commiserating about?"

He sighed. "Shaina finally admitted that she's been seeing someone else. We're done."

Kate's heart went out to him. His girlfriend, who had taken a job offer in Denver, had been growing increasingly distant and Robert had suspected that she'd met someone.

"Damn, Robbie. I'm so sorry."

He shrugged. "I won't say that it doesn't hurt like hell, but it is what it is. So, I've decided that we both need to go out, get drunk, and fuck our brains out. What do you say?"

Kate burst into laughter because there was absolutely zero attraction between her and Robert. They'd met years ago on a date and had hit it off spectacularly until their goodnight kiss. No, spark, no zing, no nothing. That's when they knew that they'd been destined to be friends.

"That sounds great," she said. "Everything but the sex, that is. Sex with you would be too close to incest."

Robert's adorable grin flashed as he gave a shudder. "You speak the truth. Okay, so eight it is. I better get to work before the boss fires me." He winked as he left, making her smile.

Kate thanked God every day for Robert. He'd saved her life after Phil's death, had kept her sane. There were times when she'd acted like a maniac, ranting and screaming, but Robert had just sat calmly with her and let her rail and give voice to her pain and anger. He'd also spent his share of nights in her bed, just holding her so she could sleep.

He'd seen her at her worst and still wanted to be her

friend, which, in her eyes, was a miracle. And now he was going to come to her rescue again.

She shied away from thoughts about Ric right then, but it was hard. He'd made her feel appreciated and alive and she'd wrecked it by getting emotional. Ric had been charming, considerate, and nothing that had gone wrong had been his fault.

As she pulled open her desk drawer to look for some aspirin, she saw the fiery desire in his blue eyes in her mind and shivered as she remembered the way his hands had felt on her skin. He'd said that he wanted to see her again, but her reaction to their lovemaking showed her that she wasn't ready for a relationship of any kind. Especially one that was supposed to be just fun.

Kate felt badly that she'd most likely hurt Ric's feelings, but she didn't know how to apologize to him or if that would even be a good idea. She'd never had one night stands even back in college, a couple of semi-serious relationships and then she'd met Phil. They had been together for three years until a blown tire ended their planned out future. That's when she'd taken the job in Coopers Creek, she had to get out of Denver.

Picking up her phone, Kate saw the time and knew that she didn't have time to sit and mope about her failed night out with Ric. Except that it hadn't been a total failure. Ric had been right about that. It had been romantic and hot until she'd weirded out over the fact that it he'd been her first since Phil. Other than that, it had been perfect and so much fun, but she couldn't think about that right now. She needed to focus on work. Blowing out a breath, Kate put on her professional persona and went to meet her first patient of the day.

*****

Ric groaned as he sat on the side of the tub taping a garbage bag around his left knee two mornings later. His back still ached from the bed-crashing incident at the cabin and he'd almost gone back to his ortho doc to have his ankle rechecked because it had hurt so much. However, he'd worked his way through the agony, taking his pain meds and keeping it elevated. The pain had finally started to subside last night, but he was still feeling the effects of it.

Ric made sure that water wouldn't get down inside the garbage bag and soak his cast. Satisfied with his handiwork, he stood up and shoved his sweat shorts down just as the bathroom door opened. He yanked them back up as Tyler entered the room.

"Dude, do you mind knocking?" Ric groused. "What if that had been Hayley?"

Tyler smirked at him. "Maybe you should lock the door."

"I can't when I'm taking a shower," Ric said. "If I fall or need help, you'll be locked out. That's why we came up with the sock on the door handle, remember?"

"Oh, yeah. Forgot. Sorry." Tyler motioned towards the bathtub as Ric took off his shorts. "Do you need help getting in?"

"No. I just plant my ass on the shower chair and swing right on in," Ric said, demonstrating. "I feel like an old geezer using that thing. What did you need?"

"I'm going to shave and Emily and Hayley are getting ready in my bathroom. I have to get on the road." Tyler commuted almost every day to Horizon's Denver office and he hated to be late. "You going to come to the meeting a little later?"

Through the miracle of modern technology, Ric and Chase attended daily board meetings via Skype, which Ric had continued doing from the Jeffries residence.

"Yeah. I'll wait until your done shaving to start the water. I don't need to scald my *cajones* when you turn on the cold water in the sink."

Tyler grinned, his gray eyes shining. "Damn. I was hoping to hear you scream like a little girl."

"Shut the hell up and give me a towel so I can at least sit here without freezing my ass off while you make yourself beautiful," Ric said.

Tyler arched a black eyebrow at him. "Would you prefer I dress like Chase?"

Ric laughed as Tyler handed him a towel. "You couldn't pull off Bermuda shorts, shades, and muscle shirts like he does."

Tyler lathered shaving cream on his face. "Yeah, and that's dressing up for him. At least we broke him of wearing that damn speedo. I swear he'd walk around naked if it wasn't illegal."

"You're right about that," Ric agreed.

Thoughts of Kate filled his head as he waited for Tyler to finish shaving. What had gone wrong? He hadn't wanted to pressure her about it, but now he was wondering if that hadn't been a mistake. Even though he'd hoped that she would, Kate hadn't called.

It shouldn't bother him, but it did. Ric was used to one-night stands, but it was obvious that Kate wasn't. After all, she'd been engaged, so she'd been in a committed relationship; something he'd never experienced. Had she just been feeling embarrassed because she wasn't used to how those sorts of encounters ended?

He was yanked back to the present when Tyler snapped his fingers in front of him.

"Wake up. I'm talking to you."

"Sorry. What?"

Tyler frowned. "What's wrong with you? You've been off for a couple of days now. Distracted."

Ric opened his mouth, but he didn't know how to frame his question. Meeting his brother-in-law's eyes, he also wondered if this would lead to an awkward conversation.

"What's the matter?" Tyler prompted.

"Can I ask you something without you getting weird about it?"

Wiping shaving cream off his jaw with a towel, Tyler nodded. "Shoot."

"Outside of Emily, have you ever had feelings for a woman? And, no, this isn't me being protective of her. You've proven how sorry you are for what you did in the past," Ric said.

Tyler smiled as he played with his wedding band. "Marrying your sister is the smartest thing I've ever done. I should've done it years ago, but I was too big of a dickhead. Anyway, the answer to your question is no. Sure, there've been some women I cared about a little bit, but I know that Emily is the only woman I'll ever love. Why do you ask?"

"How did you know?"

Tyler's smile was a trifle sad. "Because no matter how many miles were between us, I couldn't get her out of my thoughts. She was in my heart too deep. God knows I tried everything I knew to stop loving her, but I couldn't. It didn't matter how many women I slept with, they weren't the women I wanted to wake up to every morning or share my life with. Emily and I are meant to be; it's as simple as that."

Ric smiled. "I'm glad you wised up. Of course, the whipping I gave you probably knocked some sense into you."

"I deserved it, which is why I didn't fight back. So, you can't really classify it as a beat-down. What's this all about? Can it wait until tonight?"

"Yeah. Get going," Ric said. "I better get my ass in gear, too. I'll call Chase and make sure he's up."

"I'll be surprised if he's even been to bed," Tyler remarked.

"Yeah. He certainly has a habit of enjoying life to the full," Ric said.

"Yeah. Okay. I'll see you at the meeting," Tyler said.

When he'd gone, Ric turned on the water and began his shower.

*****

"I need your advice," Ric said.

He sat in Tyler and Emily's home office later that afternoon, talking to Chase over Skype. Emily had taken Hayley to the grocery store with her, so he had the house to himself. He couldn't stop thinking about Kate and he wasn't sure what to do about it.

Normally, he was in control of his emotions, but he'd felt out of sorts ever since he'd been forced to stay in Cooper's Creek. He'd moved first to Denver and then to New York so that he didn't have to be constantly reminded of Lizzie. It was especially hard staying in Tyler and Lizzie's childhood home, a place where Ric and Emily had practically grown up, too.

Memories of Lizzie were everywhere, painful memories of a woman he'd loved more than life itself. Ric would've done anything for Lizzie, but she'd fallen in love with Simon, leaving him out in the cold.

"What about?" Chase asked, his brown eyes filled with concern. For once, he was actually in his office instead of on the Rooftop headquarters. "You seem awfully serious. What gives?"

Ric cocked his head. "Can you please take out that ridiculous man-bun?"

Chase let out a shout of laughter and released his hair from its restraints. He shook out his long, deep brown hair that fell a little past his shoulders. "I lost the damn bet!"

"Bet?"

"Yeah. Smiley and I bet on how long it would be before you or Ty made me take it out. I said that it would be this morning, but Smiley said that you guys would let me get away with it until noon. I owe him two hundred bucks," Chase replied.

Ric laughed. "I'm surprised that Ty didn't say anything about it this morning, too."

"Me, too. Anyhow, what kind of advice do you need?"

"You know that I went out with Kate the other night, right?"

Chase nodded. "Yeah. How'd it go?"

A smile stole over Ric's face. "Amazing. I took her up to the Hamiltons' little cabin for dinner. I had Emily make us a romantic meal and take it over there ahead of time. We ate, drank a little wine, and talked."

"That's fantastic," Chase said. "I'm glad you hit it off."

"We did. I didn't expect to, you know? I mean, I figured

that we'd have a good time, but I didn't know that I'd end up liking her so much," Ric said.

"So, I take it that you're gonna see her again."

Ric ran a hand through his hair. "I don't know. I want to, but…"

"Uh, oh. What did you do?"

"What makes you think it was my fault?"

Chase smiled. "Because it's usually the man's fault when things go wrong with women. Naw, I'm just kidding. What happened?"

Ric felt a little uncomfortable talking about the situation, but Chase didn't have a judgmental bone in his body. He didn't make assumptions about people and always gave them the benefit of the doubt until they screwed him over. Chase also didn't shy away from talking about feelings the way a lot of guys did, which was why Ric had wanted his input on things with Kate.

He relayed the events of his evening with her to Chase and then waited for his reaction.

"Well, first off, kudos on breaking the bed," Chase said. "That's some sexy shit right there."

Ric cracked up. "It wasn't planned and now I have to get that bed replaced before they find out about it."

Chase nodded. "What exactly are you asking me, Ric?"

"Kate and I were just going to have some fun for the next few weeks, but I'm thinking that she's not that sort of woman. So, do I try to see her again, or leave it be?" Ric asked.

"Ah, it becomes clear," Chase said. "She got under your skin."

Ric felt lost. "Yeah. We've only been out twice,

but…this is the worst time for something like this to happen."

"Or maybe it's the perfect time," Chase countered. "I believe that everything happens for a reason. Maybe you were supposed to meet Kate. Are you sure it's not just because you had great sex?"

Ric drummed his fingers on the desk. "I've been asking myself the same thing. It wasn't just great, Chase. It was phenomenal. I'm talking off the Richter scale."

Chase leaned forward and put his elbows on the table where he sat. "But what made it phenomenal? Did she do something that other women haven't in the past?"

"Well, I've had a few women attack me before, but it didn't affect me the way it did when Kate did it. The thing is that I really wasn't expecting to sleep with her that night. Did the thought run across my mind? Only every five seconds, but I didn't think anything would actually happen," Ric said.

"Why not? If you'd taken any other woman up there, wouldn't you have pushed the issue of sex? I mean, convince her with your considerable powers of persuasion?" Chase asked, waggling his eyebrows.

It was true. Ric was a master at seduction and there had rarely been a woman whom he couldn't talk into bed, but he'd wanted more from Kate that night. He hadn't just suffered his way through dinner making polite conversation the way he usually did. Unlike with other women, he'd connected with Kate on more than just a physical level.

"Ric, the fact that it's taking you this long to answer my question says that you care about this woman."

Ric shook his head. "We just met. How can that be?"

"My granddaddy was the smartest person I've ever met,

Ric. I once asked him about this very topic. He told me that when it comes to love, there is no such thing as too soon or too late. Love happens in its own time, not when we think it should," Chase said.

"Love?" Ric scoffed. "Who said anything about love? I just really like Kate, that's all. It's not like I'm looking for anything serious. I'll be going back to New York in a few weeks. I don't need any entanglements."

Chase grew very sober. "Ric, if you don't think that you're in love, why are we having this conversation? As long as I've known you, you've never asked for advice about women from me, or anyone else, as far as I know. You never even asked for my advice about Lizzie and you loved her."

"How did you know?" Ric had never mentioned his attraction to Lizzie to anyone until he'd recently told Emily and Ty.

"Because I got eyes and I pick up on that kind of shit. I just never mentioned it because I could tell that you were trying to hide it," Chase said. "I figured that if you wanted anyone to know, you'd say something."

"I'm glad you didn't," Ric said. "Especially because nothing was ever going to come of my feelings for her."

"Because of Simon. I understand." Chase scratched his jaw. "Ric, you have a decision to make. You either leave things the way they are so that neither of you gets hurt when you have to go back to New York, or you see where things lead and think about the possibility of a long-distance relationship. What you're willing to do depends on how much you care for her. Seems to me like she's pretty special to have gotten you twisted up like this already."

Ric nodded. "Yeah. She is."

"In that case, don't let her get away, my friend."

Ric narrowed his eyes at Chase. "How come you haven't given serious consideration to finding someone to settle down with?"

Chase grinned. "Happy families are not for everyone. I'm not really looking for the family life. I don't think any woman would put up with my strange habits."

Ric noted the sad look that had entered Chase's eyes as if he didn't want to believe what he was saying. Chase had always said he would never have a wife or family and yet he was the one man who had such a big heart. He was great with other people's kids, and he loved Hayley to death. Something didn't ring true.

"It seems to me women flock to your strange habits. Don't let your parents' marriage cloud your judgment."

"I don't. My ass hat father is one of a kind, that's for sure. Nah, the babes like my money, nothing more."

"Partly true, but it's always you that ends the relationships so I think you're full of bull as usual. You just haven't met the right woman."

"I'm not sure there is a right woman for me. But it seems you have found one that raises the possibility of commitment. Of course, it could be Emily and Ty rubbing off on you."

Ric smiled and shook his head. "It could be. That's what I'm worried about. What if I go back to New York and find I like my life just as it is?"

Chase shrugged. "Then you'll have to let her down gently. You have to be true to yourself or it's not fair on either of you." He gave a wry smile. "Keep me posted on how things are going, good buddy."

"Thanks, good buddy. I will."

Ric hit the end button and closed the lid on his laptop. Coco had been laying at his feet, but when he turned in his chair, she stood up, wagging her tail.

"What do you think, Coco? Should I date Kate?" He ruffled her ears and scratched them for her as he looked into her light brown eyes. "You're such a pretty girl. I'm so glad you're feeling better. No more waste can scrummaging for you."

Coco wiggled her whole body and licked Ric's hands. He laughed and asked, "Do you want to go out?"

Coco cocked her head to the side for a moment and then took off running for the kitchen door. Grabbing his crutches, Ric followed Coco. A smile spread across his face as he put on his jacket and opened the door for Coco. He'd made up his mind about what to do about the stunning Dr. Donoghue and decided that a personal visit was in order.

Chapter Seven

Kate washed her hands at the sink located near the back of the exam rooms and went to meet her next patient. She opened the door, entered the exam room, and froze. Ric stood on the other side of the stainless-steel exam table, a devilish smile on his chiseled face.

"Hi, Doc."

Kate's heartbeat kicked into overdrive and her mouth went dry. He looked amazing in a pair of dark dress pants, and a red sweater worn over a white dress shirt. The vivid color suited him to a T and showed off his broad shoulders and chest.

"Hi. I think there's been a mix-up. I didn't know that I was seeing Coco today," she said, consulting the record on her tablet. "I'm supposed to be seeing a Bernese Mountain dog called Lola. He belongs to a Mr. McIntyre."

Ric laughed. "Yeah. Sorry about the subterfuge, but I lied so that I made sure I could see you. I never got your cellphone number and I didn't think your office would give it out, so I resorted to creative means to get to you."

Images of his delectable naked body flashed through Kate's mind and her body warmed even as her ire rose. "So there is no Lola?"

"Oh, there is. Lola belongs to my partner, Chase McIntyre, but they live in L.A."

She sat her tablet on the table and glared at him. "So you decided to take up valuable time that was originally intended to treat a sick animal? That appointment should've gone to a patient who needed it. This is my business, Ric. Not a place for games."

Ric sobered. "I understand that, which is why I won't take up much of your time. May I have your number so I can call you?"

Kate couldn't believe that he wanted to talk to her after what had happened between them two nights ago. "Why? Things didn't go very well the other night."

Ric came around the table, but Kate held her ground as he came to within inches of her. She tilted her head up to meet his gaze and felt her breathing quicken as she looked into his eyes.

"I respectfully disagree, Kate. Things went incredibly well until something upset you. I'd like to talk to you about what happened, but in private," he said.

Kate didn't want to talk about it, but she knew that he deserved some sort of explanation.

"Kate, I think we moved a little fast," Ric said. "I know we talked about having fun together, but maybe we need to just slow things down a bit."

Kate looked down and took a step back. "You can't undo

what happened, Ric. I don't think I can do this. You should go."

Ric advanced on her again. "Kate, I know we can't take it back and I don't want to. It was hot and fun and I don't want to erase it. I sure as hell won't forget breaking that bed."

Kate giggled and covered her face. She couldn't deny that it was funny, nor could she deny that being with Ric had been one of the most intense experiences in her life. "Neither will I, but the fact that the sex was incredible doesn't mean that we should see each other again."

Ric nodded. "You're right. Kate, I won't lie to you. Most of my romantic life has been a string of one-night stands and brief affairs. My work life is hectic and getting tied up with someone wasn't high on my list of priorities. But then we met and I really like you. I want you, especially after the other night, and I want to spend time together and get to know you better. I get you have doubts but so do I. I don't want to keep you, so can I call you tonight to talk about all of this?"

Ric's honesty and consideration of her touched Kate and she couldn't resist his coaxing smile. "All right. Give me your phone."

His triumphant grin made her laugh as he put his phone in her hand. It was warm from his palm and the memory of the way his hands felt on her bare skin made her mess up a couple of times. Finally, she got it right, gave his phone back, and put his number in her phone, too.

Ric said, "Call me when it's convenient for you. I don't have any plans tonight, so it makes no difference to me what time you call."

She couldn't resist teasing him. "So you'll be waiting with bated breath?"

His deep laugh gave her goosebumps. "Not sure about bated breath, but I'll be waiting."

"Okay."

Kate opened the door to the waiting room for him. When he drew even with her, he stopped and gave her a lingering look full of heat before continuing on his way. As she shut the door, Kate leaned against it until her nerves had calmed down a bit. The man was almost overwhelming.

Since her next appointment wouldn't be there for another half hour, Kate went to Robert's office. He was on the phone, but pointed to an empty chair, inviting her to sit. She did and crossed her legs. Nervous energy made her legs bounce until she saw Robert's raised eyebrow. She stopped and gave him an apologetic smile.

Robert gave her a curious look as he hung up. "What's up?"

"Ric came to see me. He wants me to call him tonight to talk about things," she said and filled him in on the rest of their conversation. "What do you think?"

Leaning back in his chair, Robert thoughtfully scratched the back of his head. "I think he's smart for seeing what a great woman you are and I like that he's suggesting to slow things down. I don't want you to get hurt. You've had enough pain to last a lifetime."

Kate rolled her eyes. "I know that, but what do you think I should do?"

"It all depends on what you want out of a relationship with Ric. I think that it would be a big mistake to get serious. He lives in New York. The type of vet work in New York is not really what you enjoy. And what about the Alpine Rescue Club? You've always lived in Colorado."

Defiantly she uttered. "Perhaps it's time for a change. You're right, I've never really lived anywhere else"

"So you want this thing with Ric to be serious?"

"I didn't say that. I'm not getting serious, I'm just asking if you think I should see where things go?"

"Katie, he's going back to New York. Where do you think they're going to go?"

Kate took offense to his hard tone. "Don't treat me like a child, Robert. People do have long-distanced relationships that work. Plus, I'd be perfectly happy just seeing him once a month or something like that. I don't have time for a committed relationship, but something casual like that would be perfect."

Robert sighed as he looked around his messy office. "I'm sorry. I'm not trying to put a damper on your fun, but he's the first guy since Phil and you were upset about sleeping with him when you went out the other night."

Kate nodded. "I know and I'm still somewhat nervous, but I also had so much fun with Ric and I need some fun, Robert. I'm tired of being sad and angry. I think I'm finally ready to start living again and Ric seems like the right guy to do that with."

"Well, he is rich, so he has that going for him," Robert said.

Kate frowned. "He's rich? I know that he has a business in New York, but I didn't know that he's rich."

Robert shook his head. "I'm always telling you that you need to pay more attention to gossip. He's one of Tyler Jeffries' partners. Their company is the one that just bought the hospital. Ric runs their New York division and their other partner runs the L.A. office."

"Chase McIntyre?"

"Yeah. They all grew up here," Robert said. "They started an investment firm in New York as soon as they graduated from college and the rest is history. So, he could afford to fly you to New York for a weekend or something."

Kate laughed. "I'm not going to be a kept woman."

"I think that you just made up your mind about Ric," Robert said.

"I guess I did," she said. "And now I have to stop acting like a college girl and go be a vet. Thanks, Robbie. I really appreciate it."

She went around the desk and hugged Robert.

"You're welcome. Now get going. Some of us have work to do," he quipped, shooing her out of his office.

*****

Settling on the couch that evening with Cinders, one of her four pets, Kate took a few moments to decompress before calling Ric. The black Scottish Terrier nudged her hand with a damp nose and she pet his silky head. He'd been Phil's dog and had been as lost without him as she'd been. Since then, Cinders had been her constant companion whenever she was home and had been a great source of comfort to her.

Taking a deep breath, Kate dialed Ric's number.

"Hi, Doc. How was the rest of your day?"

Kate was glad that he couldn't see her big smile. "It was busy, as usual, but I was able to get out of there at a reasonable time."

"Glad to hear it."

"So, I heard something about you that you didn't tell me

the other night," she said.

"It's not true. I swear."

"Then you're really not rich?"

His laugh sounded in her ear. "Okay, I take that back. Yes, I am, and I make no apologies for it. What else did you hear about me?"

"That your company is the one that bought the hospital."

"That's right. I assume that you know about Hayley's injury last year?"

"Yes, Emily told me about it. You must've all been terrified," Kate said. "Post-concussion syndrome can be severe and there are still varying opinions as to how many long-lasting effects it can have."

"Yeah. It was a tough time. Hayley's always been so funny and full of life. Seeing her so sick was horrible. But, she's doing great, as you know. After she was hurt, Ty told us that he wanted to buy the medical center and expand it. He was upset because they had to take Hayley to Denver for a peds neuro specialist since we didn't have one.

"There are a lot of specialists that we need around here, but without the proper funding, the hospital couldn't afford to bring them on board. So, since we have the means, we figured that we could help the people of our hometown by improving the healthcare around here," Ric said.

Kate's estimation of Ric went up. There was a lot more substance behind him than she'd thought. "That's really kind of you all."

"Well, none of us had the best childhoods. Ty's dad ended up dying in prison when he and his sister, Lizzie, were just teenagers. Same for me and Emily. I was fourteen when Mom passed. Ty's mom, Maggie, became a sort of surrogate mother to us, and to a lot of kids in town."

"What about your father?"

Ric snorted. "He fell apart after Mom died and drank himself into oblivion every night and eventually pickled his liver. I basically finished raising Emily. He drank away most of our money, so I worked at the Hamiltons and one of the cattle ranches outside of town to make ends meet. If it wasn't for Maggie having me and Em over for supper a few nights a week, we'd have gone hungry sometimes."

"I'm so sorry. I had no idea." Kate admired him for taking care of a younger sister when he'd been just a kid himself.

"It's okay. It made me more driven to succeed in life and it taught me a great work ethic. It hasn't been easy, but we've all pulled ourselves up by the bootstraps. We became each other's family," Ric told her.

Kate played with one of Cinders' front paws. "That's great. I've met Tyler. He can be a little…intense."

Ric laughed. "To say the least. He's a real bastard when it comes to business, but he's a pushover with the people he loves. He has a pretty short fuse and he and I butt heads a lot, much like brothers do."

Kate was putting the dynamic of Ric's relationships together. "What about Chase? You mentioned him, but how does he fit into the picture with your group?"

Ric's laughter surprised her. "I'm sorry. You have to meet Chase to fully appreciate him. He's the exact opposite of me and Ty. Footloose and fancy free. He's loyal, kind to a fault, and hates wearing clothes. He makes us sick because he's one of those people who's good at everything and everyone loves him. He's hard to explain."

"He's good at everything? Like what?"

"You name it, he's good at it."

Kate decided to test him. "Singing?"

"Sings, plays guitar, and tinkers around on piano. He was our best receiver in high school, he's a great dancer, and he knows his way around a kitchen. He draws, likes to write poetry, and loves to play just about any sport," Ric said.

"Wow. He sounds like quite the guy. Perhaps I *should* meet him," she teased.

"Right now I'm really glad he's in LA."

"Well, I'm not interested in anyone who lives in LA."

Who she *might* be interested in hung in the air like a balloon about to be popped.

Ric said, "Glad to hear it." Then his voice turned seductive. "Does this qualify as a phone date?"

Talking to Ric was so easy that they'd slipped into conversation before she'd meant to. "I guess so," she said, chuckling.

"All right. I hate to ruin the mood, but I need you to tell me what upset you so much the other night."

Her stomach tightened with nerves. She'd known that he would ask, but that didn't make telling him any easier. "Do you remember the day at the Diner when I said that I hadn't been out with anyone since Phil died?"

"Yeah, I remember."

Kate fidgeted with Cinders' collar. "What I meant was that I haven't dated anyone since then. At all. You're the first man I've...been intimate with since him." Silence met her quiet announcement and she checked to see if Ric was still on the line. "Ric?"

"I'm here. I wish you would've told me, Kate. We'd

have taken things a lot slower. That's a big step, you know?"

His kind tone of voice brought tears to Kate's eyes. "I've been thinking about that a lot. I think I didn't mention it because I didn't want to overthink it. I didn't want to feel nervous or scared. I just wanted to feel alive and free and you certainly made me feel those things."

"You could've had that with any guy you wanted to. What made me different, Kate?"

Kate must have asked herself that question a thousand times and she still didn't have a definitive answer. "I can't really explain it, Ric. All I can say is that you're the first man who's caught my attention since Phil. You did the first day we met and I couldn't resist you the day you invited me to lunch."

"And I couldn't get you out of my mind," Ric said. "That said, do you still want to see me?"

The hope in his voice was endearing. "Yes. Still the same rules though. Just something light and fun?"

"Definitely. Light and fun. And any time you want to break another bed, just let me know."

Kate laughed and Cinders barked. "Shh."

"Who's that?"

"My dog, Cinders. He's a very handsome Scottish Terrier and my best friend," she said.

"I'll bet he's cute."

"Well, I'm sure you'll meet him," she said.

"I look forward to it. So, what are you doing Friday night?"

"Actually, I'm going away for the weekend. My best friend and I are going kayaking. I'd invite you along, but..."

Ric chuckled. "One broken ankle is enough, thanks. I

hope you guys have a great time."

"We always do. I'd say that we could get together tomorrow night, but I hold evening hours every Thursday night and it's usually pretty late until I get done at the clinic," she said.

"Yeah. Tomorrow doesn't work for me, either. I have to go to Denver for a meeting and we most likely won't get back to town until late," Ric told her regretfully. "We'll just shoot for next week. No sweat."

Kate was disappointed, too, but she'd been looking forward to kayaking and she wasn't going to change her plans. "Right."

"Well, I'm going to let you go so that you can get some rest, but I'll give you a call tomorrow, okay?"

"Sounds good. Have a good night."

"You, too. Don't go breaking any beds without me."

"Get off the phone, Stanford," she said and laughed when the phone went dead in her ear.

Chapter Eight

Ric sat going over expense spreadsheets at a small conference table in Tyler's office at their Denver headquarters the next afternoon. He had his ankle propped up on a chair on the opposite side of the table. Tyler stormed into his office and slammed the door shut, causing Ric to jump and bang his cast on the bottom of the table.

"Jesus H. Christ, Ty!" he shouted as his ankle throbbed. "What the hell's wrong with you?"

"I'm going to kill him. I swear I will."

The fury in Tyler's stormy gray eyes alarmed Ric. "Who are you talking about and what did they do?"

"Chase sent the McKnight's the marketing material for their debenture offer without sign off and I've just had a very pissed off Doug McKnight on the phone."

Ric sighed. Chase was never one to play by the rules and often forgot to get the material signed off by all three of them before approaching the clients with his often out of the box ideas. It took Ty and Ric to reign in Chase's creativity. Often Ric was needed to position whatever madcap idea Chase came up with.

"How pissed was McKnight? Enough for us to lose this deal?" Raising over five hundred million in one deal would be a very nice fat commission for the firm but if they lost the deal after so much fanfare their reputations would be in tatters.

"We have to fly out and see McKnight in Seattle and ensure we do damage control." Tyler shook his head and sobered. "I feel like a major shit. I called and bitched him out in a voicemail."

Ric groaned. "Ty, why do you always jump the gun like that? You should've waited for me. You know I handle Chase better than you. I love his creative side and we just need him to understand that we are here to temper his off the wall ideas when it's needed."

Tyler dropped heavily into a chair. "One of our biggest investors, Ric. If we lost McKnight, the market would soon know why, and the word would spread. We still don't know the full fallout from this. We have to do damage control. And the fact remains that he didn't consult us. We always decide this stuff together. He knows that."

Ric, the most reasonable of the partners, went into mediator mode. "I know, but let's just see what happens before we panic. We'll talk to Chase about ensuring this doesn't happen again without our knowledge, and we can fly and visit McKnight. That should show how serious we are and pacify his ego."

"Yeah, you're right." Tyler smiled. "I have to admit I may have overreacted."

Ric laughed. "We raise more money for our clients because of Chase's creativity, let's not forget that."

"True," Tyler said as his phone rang again. "It's Chase."

He put it on speaker and they were treated to a ten-minute tirade from Chase about Tyler's voicemail, during which Tyler managed to remain calm. Ric alternated between being amused at some of the inventive names Chase called Tyler and concerned by Chase's erratic speech pattern.

When he'd finally run out of steam, Tyler asked, "Are you done?"

"Yeah, I guess, you fuckerbitch."

Ric's jaw tensed as he fought down a laugh.

Tyler smiled. "Well, there's a new one."

"Nah. The kids are saying it now."

"Look, Chase, I'm sorry. It's just that this deal will cement our place as one of the bigger investment firms. Any chance of it going wrong and our reputation and profit goes down the drain," Tyler said.

"So you said in your bitch-mail," Chase retorted. "I'm sure Ric the Fixer can get McKnight to stay. Besides, if McKnight would pull his head out of his ass for one minute he'd see it's a winner campaign."

Ric was impressed. "I must say having gone over it while you boys ranted at each other I think you're right."

"No worries."

Tyler said, "Chase, please don't do something like this again without our sign off? I know you don't like rules but they are there for a reason."

"I was going to, but I told my P.A. the wrong send out date. It wasn't supposed to go to McKnight until *next* Thursday after you guys had seen it. My bad."

Tyler put a hand over his mouth and walked away from the table.

"Uh, Chase, that's a pretty big mistake. What's up? Is everything all right?" Ric asked.

"Just some family troubles. Can't you cut me some slack? I realize that I ain't perfect like you and Tyler." They heard Chase sigh. "Never mind. I got work to do."

"Chase," Ric began.

"Sorry, it's been a bad week. I'll try not to fuck up in the future."

He hung up and Ric and Tyler exchanged somber glances.

"Maybe I could've handled it a little differently, but you know that I'm not wrong about this," Tyler said. "Screwing up a launch date isn't a little mistake."

Ric blew out a breath. "Yeah. I know. Well, we've dealt with worse. It's just a matter of doing some damage control. Speaking of which, I'll book a flight to Seattle."

As Tyler started discussing their strategy to save this deal, Ric had the feeling that it was going to be a very long weekend.

****

As Kate rode home with Robert on Sunday afternoon, she looked at her cellphone for the hundredth time, but there was no answering text from Ric yet. They'd talked briefly Thursday when he'd called her, but she hadn't heard from him since then, so she'd sent him a text that morning. He'd said that they'd been dealing with a work emergency, so she hoped that was the reason why he hadn't answered her.

"No word from lover boy, huh?"

Kate narrowed her eyes at Robert. "Shut up. I was

checking email."

"Mmm hmm. Sure you were."

"You know what you need, Robert?"

Robert glanced at her. "What?"

"A new girlfriend."

Robert laughed and took the next exit, which would take them to the road that was the back way to Cooper's Creek. "No, I think I'm better off single right now. I have to get my sea legs under me again before I get involved with someone again."

"I know that feeling. But your situation is a lot different than mine. And you weren't together very long before she bailed."

Robert gave her an irritated look. "That's not helpful. I realize that I didn't hold her interest. I don't need you to point that out to me."

Kate rubbed his shoulder. "That's not what I meant. She didn't deserve you, Robbie. You're a fantastic guy. You're sexy, smart, and you have a kind heart. If she couldn't see all that about you, then it's her loss. You'll find somebody much better."

He shook his head. "How did my question turn into you consoling me, even though I don't need it?"

Kate laughed. "Because I don't want you lecturing me about Ric."

Robert grinned. "I'm just practicing my Dr. Phil routine, that's all."

"Well, I don't need you playing Dr. Phil any more than you need me to console you. Got it?" Kate asked.

"Yes, ma'am!" Robert saluted her.

Her text message alert went off and Kate almost squealed

when she saw that it was from Ric. However, she kept her excitement inside as she clicked on it.

Ric: Hi Doc. Sorry I didn't get back to you until now. It's been a nightmare of a weekend.
Kate: That's ok. Sorry to hear that.
Ric: Did you have fun?
Kate: Yeah.
Ric: Good.
Kate: Are you still in Denver?
Ric: No. On the way home.
Kate: Me too.

Kate bit her lip in indecision. It would be more prudent for her to unpack and get ready for the week ahead, but she really wanted to see Ric.

Kate: Would you like to come over and watch a movie tonight? I make great popcorn.
Ric: Sounds great. I'll bring the beer. What time?
Kate: Seven?
Ric: Ok. What's your address?

Kate sent it to him, trying not to grin like a school girl.

Ric: Got it. See ya then. ☺

Feeling wicked, Kate texted: *Know what? Instead of watching a movie, I'd like to see if we could break my bed.*

Ric: LOL That can be arranged. I'll still bring beer.

Kate: And I'll still make popcorn.

Ric: Ok, I'll bring chocolate sundaes

Kate: That could get messy if they melt

Ric: Best we watch movie naked then so if you spill it's easier for me to lick off

Kate's imagination went into overdrive and she hoped that her cheeks weren't pink.

Ric: ??

Kate: Only if you buy me new sheets.

Ric: Deal! See ya at 7.

Kate: See ya! ☺

"I take it from that silly smile that that was lover boy."

Kate laughed. "Yes, it was. He's coming over to watch a movie tonight."

Robert grinned. "I guess you'll be in late to work tomorrow since you're having a sleepover."

She smacked his arm. "We're just watching a movie."

"Like hell. It might start out that way, but you'll wind up in the bedroom."

"Shows what you know. We'll just watch the movie in bed, then we'll already be there."

Robert cracked up. "Good idea. Economize your time, and, hey, if you watch a porno, you can do it all at once."

"We're not going to watch a porno. Ric gets me hot all on his own. He's better than any porn star."

"Okay, okay." Robert put up a hand to stop her. "Enough. I'm officially done with this conversation."

Kate sent him a cheeky grin. "I thought you might say that."

Robert steered the topic back to kayaking for the rest of

the trip home.

Chapter Nine

"You can't drive."

Ric scowled at Emily as they stood in the kitchen of the big farmhouse that evening. "Yes, I can. Your car is automatic, so I only need my right foot. And I haven't taken any pain meds since Tylenol seems to be doing the trick. There's no reason I can't drive now. Please let me borrow your car."

Worry creased Emily's forehead. "What if something happens and you have an accident?"

Ric's expression softened. "Em, nothing is going to happen. I'm a big boy. I can handle this. Please?"

Emily relented and took her car keys off one of the hooks by the door. "Okay, but be careful."

Ric took them and kissed her cheek. "Thanks, sis. Don't wait up."

Emily smiled and shook her head as she opened the door for him. He swung his way out to her car and opened the door. Unbeknownst to Emily, Ric had already had Tyler deposit the beer in Emily's car. Tyler still drove Ric's Hummer, affectionately named The Beast, because Ric couldn't get up in the vehicle at the moment. Therefore, Emily's car was the only transportation Ric had.

Ric put his crutches over on the passenger seat, sat down, and swung his legs in. He had to move the seat back to accommodate his long legs, but otherwise it felt fine. After settling in, he turned the ignition and waved at Emily, who stood outside the kitchen door with a concerned expression. She gave him a little wave and he put the car in gear.

It felt good to drive again and Ric turned up the radio. Emily loved 80's music and Bon Jovi sang *Living on a Prayer* as he went down the road. Ric reflected on the weekend spent sorting through the mess that Chase's lapse in judgment had caused. McKnight chewed their asses off but Ric worked his charm, calming him down and talking numbers that McKnight could not ignore.

However, to their horror, word of their cockup had started doing the rounds and confidence in the firm was dented. They had a few clients rumbling about leaving.

Tyler, the financial wiz of the three of them, had crunched numbers, going through every possible scenario to prepare them for the result of possible fallout. But the biggest problem was that the Villanova Group, another one of their biggest accounts, who was talking about severing ties with them, which would place them in jeopardy.

Chase had pissed Tyler off by sending a smart ass email that contained his complete itinerary for the next three months so that they were aware of his every move. Ric hadn't let on to Tyler, for fear he'd blow a gasket, but the fact that Chase had put "take a shit" at 6:30 a.m. every day, had amused the hell out of him.

He wouldn't answer their calls or emails, but the one he'd sent them said that he would attend the Denver office meeting on Monday morning at 8 a.m. Ric wasn't happy with Chase for not responding to them, but Ric knew it was probably problems with Chase's sister that sent him off the rails.

Tyler was giving Chase space, but he told Ric that if he didn't get satisfaction at the board meeting on Monday, he was getting on a plane to L.A. to deal with Chase in person.

As he pulled up in front of Kate's house, Ric let go of all that, though. He was mentally drained and keyed up at once. Spending time with Kate would be the perfect way to relax for a few hours. He carefully got out of the Subaru and grabbed his crutches. He hobbled to the rear seat and retrieved the six-pack of Bud.

Slowly, so he didn't shake the beer up, he made his way to Kate's door, admiring the two-story gray stone house with white shutters. There were a couple of big maple trees in the yard and the property was nicely landscaped. He rang the doorbell and heard dogs bark.

Kate opened the door and three pooches of various sizes swarmed around Ric.

"Hi," she said. "Come on in." She grabbed the beer from him, and made the dogs move back and stay down so that Ric could pass through the doorway. "I should've put them in their kennels. Sorry about that."

Ric smiled as he looked at the Scottish terrier, chocolate Lab, and Great Dane. "That big one won't eat me, will he?"

Kate laughed. "No. Daisy is afraid of her own shadow.

I'm surprised that she hasn't run and hidden by now."

He pointed to the beer. "I kept my end of the bargain."

Her luscious mouth curved upwards and Ric was hit by a longing to kiss her and never stop. "I'll go start the popcorn. Come have a seat in the living room."

Following her, Ric took notice of the warm earth tones of her furnishings. The décor didn't follow any one theme, instead being a hodge-podge of various styles. The living room was done in a light green with white trim. A sand colored couch and matching recliners arranged around a large square oak wood coffee table created an inviting seating area.

A couple of pet beds and a cat condo were situated in a far corner next to the large bay window and several large prints depicting various foreign locales hung on the walls.

"Make yourself comfortable," Kate said, motioning towards the couch.

Ric sat down and looked for a place to put his crutches.

Kate said, "Here, I'll take those and your jacket."

He shrugged out of it and handed it to her. "Thanks. Oh, I also held up my other end of the bargain." He grinned at her as he held out a small box that he'd taken out of his jacket pocket.

She gave him a suspicious look. "What did you do?"

"Open it."

She lifted the lid and took out the Macy's gift card.

"You can buy whatever sheets strike your fancy," he said.

Kate blushed as she laughed and Ric thought she had the best laugh he'd ever heard. It was a rich, slightly throaty sound that made him happy just hearing it. "I don't believe you. I thought you were just joking."

"Oh, no. I never joke about bargains. It's important to

always come through on your end," Ric said.

Kate leaned down to kiss his cheek and the scent of her vanilla and jasmine perfume hit him. He wanted to pull her down on the couch and have her for a snack instead of the popcorn, but he behaved and resisted that urge.

"I'll be right back."

Ric watched her walk from the room and thought that jeans would always be the clothing he liked best on her. Next to her birthday suit, that was. "Down, boy," he said to his libido.

*****

Kate fixed a tray of snacks and beer as she listened to Ric get acquainted with the dogs. She smiled at the way he kept trying to coax Daisy closer. It amused her that he was so persistent and figured that he must be the same way in his business dealings to have become such a success.

Finished, she carried the tray of popcorn, nachos, and cookies into the living room. "I was hungry for a little more than popcorn."

"What is all that?" Ric asked as she sat the tray on the coffee table. "Nachos? I love nachos. How'd you know?"

Kate handed him a beer. "I don't know. You just seem like a nachos kind of guy to me."

Ric twisted the top off the bottle and took a pull from it. "Well, I am. I'm a junk food nut period, which is why I have to limit myself and go to the gym since I don't do ranch work anymore."

"I can see that you take very good care of yourself," Kate said sitting down by him.

"Thanks. I try. You take good care of yourself, too."

Their eyes met and Kate's stomach dropped pleasantly as

their evening of passion came back to her. Not that it was ever far from her thoughts. "Thanks. What would you like to watch? An action movie? Horror?"

Ric smiled and she wanted to kiss him so badly that she almost attacked him again. "Actually, I'm going to let in on a little secret that no one knows. I'm trusting you with very sensitive material, here."

His playful comment made her chuckle. "Okay. I won't tell a soul. Scout's honor."

"All right, but if this gets into the wrong hands, I'm going to have to punish you," he said.

"I promise."

Ric looked a trifle bashful as he said, "I'm a secret romantic and my favorite movie of all time is *Someone Like You*. I've probably watched it a hundred times, but it never gets old."

Kate couldn't hide her smile. "Really? A big, tough guy like you is into romantic movies? I had you pegged for Jason Bourne or James Bond. Vin Diesel, maybe."

"I like all of them, but I'm a sucker for a happy ending." He laughed. "That didn't come out the way I meant it to."

Kate giggled at his poor word choice. "I knew what you meant. I think it's sweet that you're in touch with your softer side."

"But remember, you can't tell anyone."

"So you want to watch Someone Like You?"

"Do you like it?"

Kate gave him a sidelong glance as she put the TV on and brought up Netflix. "I don't think that there are many women who don't. Hugh Jackman!"

Ric popped a nacho into his mouth and crunched it.

"Mmm. Spicy. Love it. We have an audience."

"Oh, I forgot to introduce you. That little guy is Cinders and the Lab is Rocco. And I already told you about Daisy," Kate said. "I have a parrot named Manny, too."

"Yes, you did. How come she's so shy?"

The brindle Great Dane sat just inside the doorway of the living room, warily watching Ric.

"She was a shelter dog and was abused by her previous owners. I took her and she's starting to come around, but it's been hard," Kate said.

"Aw, poor baby," Ric said. "Those are the kind of people I'd like to beat the shit out of. Give them a taste of their own medicine."

"Me, too."

Ric reached for a bowl, but Kate caught his wrist at the last second. "You don't want those. They're dog treats."

He looked at the bowl and then back at her. "They are? They look like Fritos."

"Looks can be deceiving. I give them to the dogs when I have snacks so that they don't feel left out, but so they're getting something that's good for them."

"That's really nice of you." Ric picked up one of the treats and sniffed it experimentally. "Smells pretty good. Dare me?"

Kate giggled when he opened his mouth and acted like he was going to eat it. "They're not bad, actually."

"You've eaten them?"

"I try all of the treats we sell. How else will I know if they're spicy?" she said, shrugging.

Ric looked at the treat. "Is that a bad thing?"

"If a dog eats or drinks too much or too fast at a time, it

can make them sick to their stomach. Spicy treats will make them drink much more than they should at one time, especially because owners sometimes give them too many treats," Kate said.

"Do they taste good?"

"Those are chicken and they're not half bad. I don't sit around eating them, of course, but I did try them when we first got them."

"If I eat it will you rub my tummy?"

"Absolutely."

Ric studied the treat and sniffed it again. "Okay."

He popped the treat into his mouth and chewed thoughtfully. Slowly, his face registered distaste and Kate dissolved into giggles.

"I thought you said that these weren't half bad?" he commented around the treat. He took a huge swig of beer to wash the treat down.

Kate laughed so hard that she snorted. Tears gathered in her eyes as Ric shoved a nacho in his mouth and chewed it quickly. He followed it by more beer and then belched, which set Kate off on another laughing jag.

"God, that was the shittiest thing I've ever tasted!" He looked at the dogs. "You can have my share. I don't know how you eat those things." His hand shot out and he grabbed Kate's arm. "And you're going to pay. You never ate any of them did you?" he accused as he dragged her over onto his lap and started tickling her.

Kate squealed. "Yes! Yes, I did! I swear!"

"Hey! Shit!"

Kate suddenly found herself dumped on the floor between the coffee table and the couch as a horrible snarl and growl filled the room, followed by Ric's shout of pain. Kate scrambled to her feet and saw that Daisy had Ric's left bicep clamped in her huge jaws.

"Daisy! Drop!" she commanded, her heart pounding.

Ric held up a hand. "Don't shout. Damn, that hurts." His voice was soft even though it held fear and pain. "Daisy, it's okay, honey. I was just playing around. I wasn't going to hurt Kate, I promise. I would never hurt your mommy."

Kate couldn't believe that he was trying to reassure Daisy when he was the one being attacked.

"It's all right, girl," he continued. "See? Your mommy's okay. We were just fooling around."

Daisy growled when he reached his free hand towards her.

"Ric, don't."

"Shh. You're such a pretty girl, such a good girl. You're not mean. You just want to protect Kate. That's your job. But you're killing my arm. Drop, Daisy. Let me go. I'm not going to hurt anyone."

Ric kept talking to the huge dog and her tail started to wag. He slowly laid his free hand on her head and scratched behind her ears, making her tail wag faster. Her grip on his arm loosened and she released him, but Ric kept scratching her ears and petting her head. Daisy shocked them both by giving him a big, sloppy kiss and laying down on the floor.

"Oh, my God. Are you all right? Did she break the skin? I'm so sorry," Kate said as Ric flopped back against the couch.

"No, she didn't break the skin. Felt like a vise grip on my arm, though. It's okay. She was just scared that I was going to hurt you. Otherwise, she would've never come near me,"

Ric said.

"Take off your shirt so I can look at your arm." She lifted his Dale Earnhardt sweatshirt up and helped him take it off.

Ric leaned towards her and she examined his injured arm. Although there were indentations in it, Daisy's teeth hadn't actually punctured his skin. It was starting to bruise already, though.

"That's going to be sore." Kate was mortified. "I'm so sorry. She's never done anything like that before."

"It's all right. I'm a stranger and, to her, it looked like I was hurting you," Ric said. "I'm not mad. At least now you know that she'd go after anyone who tried to break in here."

"Yeah, I guess so. Make sure you put ice on that when you get home," Kate said.

"Perhaps you could get me some now? I can leave it on while we watch the movie."

Kate stared at him. "You still want to stay?"

Ric rubbed her shoulder consolingly. "Of course. Kate, I've been kicked, bitten, and tossed on my ass by horses and bulls. I can handle a little dog bite. She really wasn't being mean."

Kate gave him a tremulous smile. "Not many people would realize that."

"Well, I've worked around animals all my life. Even when I came home from college in the summers, I worked on the ranches or farms to make money," Ric said. "So don't worry about me. I've had a lot worse."

Kate shook her head. "I still feel terrible."

Ric leaned over and kissed her. "Don't. I'm fine. You examined me. What's your assessment, Doc? Will I live?" He took her hand and put it over his heart. "Does that feel normal to you?"

Kate glanced at Daisy, but she was completely uninterested in what they were doing. "Amazing."

"I've been told that."

Kate ran her hand over his nipple and he sucked in a breath. "You *are* amazing, but I was referring to Daisy. She doesn't care now that you're touching me."

Ric looked at the dog. "You're right. She must know that I'm her friend now. Kate, if you keep doing that, there's not going to be any movie."

Kate had kept playing with his chest, enjoying his hard muscles and warm skin. She didn't want to stop touching him and she loved seeing the desire in his eyes. "We could always go watch something in bed."

Chapter Ten

Kate's statement made Ric's blood pump harder through his veins and her roving hand was driving him crazy. His jeans were getting tighter by the second.

"The only thing I want to watch in bed is you," he confessed. "Can that be arranged?"

"I think it can. Let me just get rid of all this so that the dogs don't eat it and I'll be right back," Kate said, rising.

When she left the room, Ric took out a roll of breath mints and popped one in his mouth. He didn't want to kiss her with dog treat and beer breath. Crunching up the mint, he reached down and patted Daisy's head. She licked his hand and thumped her tail. The other dogs came to be petted, too, now that the drama was over and Ric played with all of them until Kate returned. She ushered the dogs into the big room attached to the laundry, which held their beds and gave them access to the yard. The laundry door locked like a back door, leaving the room she'd had built on with the ability to have a stable door, the bottom half open, for Daisy and the other dogs to get into the quarter acre yard to do their business.

She gave him his crutches and he stood up.

"Follow me," Kate said.

"Right behind your sweet behind, honey," he said.

Kate smiled and led the way to the stairs. Ric's strength made it easy to hop his way up to the second floor. It was as nice as the rest of the house. The hallway was lined with all kinds of pictures, which Ric assumed were family and friends. At the end of the hallway, Kate opened a set of double doors into the master bedroom.

It had a cozy atmosphere with more earth tones and warm colors. He didn't notice more than that because Kate was turning down the bed. His attention centered on her as she came back to him. Her dark hair gleamed in the low light of the one lamp she'd turned on and her eyes glowed with desire.

Just thinking about what awaited him under her clothes made Ric harder and he was glad that he'd picked up some jeans with a more relaxed fit to accommodate his cast. They accommodated his raging hard-on, too.

"Why don't you come over here and get comfortable?" She patted the bed.

"Okay." He complied and pulled her down beside him. "You are so beautiful, Kate. I've been thinking about this since last week."

"Me, too," she said as he cupped her cheek. "I want you, Ric."

"I want you, too. I want to touch you, kiss you everywhere."

Ric took her lips in a kiss filled with raw hunger,

delving his tongue into her mouth to tease hers. Closing his arms around her, he ignored the painful dog bite as she embraced him and kissed him back. She tasted so good and felt so right in his arms and he forced himself to slow down.

He wanted to savor Kate this time and give her as much pleasure as possible. She played with his hair and goosebumps broke out over his back. Carefully so he didn't hit her with his cast, he laid her back and continued kissing her. He slowly caressed her toned midriff over her stomach and brought his hand up to cup one of her breasts.

She moaned into his mouth and kissed him harder. Her nipple grew tight under his palm and he brushed his thumb over it through her T-shirt. The little whimper in the back of her throat sent his body temperature soaring. Grasping the bottom hem of her shirt, he pulled it up and over her head.

The red satin bra she wore was the perfect complement for her creamy skin. His mouth left hers to trail kisses along her jaw to her throat. Kate gasped when he bit her and he chuckled against her skin. He released the front clasp of her bra and parted it.

"God, Kate, you have the most beautiful breasts I've ever seen," he told her. "They're perfect."

She smiled. "I doubt that, but I'm glad you like them."

Kneading one, he said, "I love them. I could play with them for hours."

"I don't think I could take waiting for hours, Ric. God that feels so good."

Ric leaned over and took the nipple of the one he wasn't playing with in his mouth, running his tongue around the stiff peak. Kate moved restlessly, her breathing coming quicker. He groaned as he lightly pinched her nipple and her back arched.

Searing heat shot to his groin over her restless movements and Ric desperately needed to get rid of his jeans. Reluctantly removing his hands and mouth from her body, Ric rolled until he was on his back so he could undo his jeans.

Kate rolled over to him and brushed his hands away. "Allow me to do the honors."

He smiled and put his arms behind his head. "Yes, ma'am."

Watching her unfasten and unzip them excited him even more. She urged him to lift his hips and drew his jeans down over his legs. Careful of his cast, she removed them and let them drop to the floor.

Ric growled when she ran her hand over the bulge in his black boxer-briefs. Raising his head, he watched her pull them down, freeing his hard cock. She ran the tip of her tongue up the underside of his shaft to the tip and Ric moaned low in his chest as pleasure traveled along his nerve endings.

When she took him in her pretty mouth, he couldn't hold still. He made little thrusts as she swirled her tongue around him.

"Mmm, that feels so good, baby," he murmured.

Ric knew that some women didn't like doing that, but Kate seemed to be enjoying herself. However, he wasn't about to let her unman him.

"Honey, you are very talented at that, but I don't want the show to be over too soon."

Kate released him and gave him a wicked smiled. "We definitely don't want that."

He reached for her, but she scooted off the bed and stood up. Slowly, she got completely rid of her bra, drawing the straps down her arms before letting the lingerie drop to the floor. Then she undid the snap of her jeans and parted them. Ric grew even harder as he watched her perform a strip tease for him.

"You're killing me, Kate," he said when she kicked her jeans aside and bent over with her ass towards him.

Kate giggled and hooked her fingers in the elastic sides of the satin panties that matched her bra and slid them down over her sexy legs. Ric's need for her soared as she shook her rear at him. Then she crawled on the bed with him and he practically dragged her over to him so he could kiss her.

*****

Kate loved the way Ric kissed. He was thorough yet he didn't kiss her hard enough to crush her mouth. She cupped his head and met his tongue, stroking hers against it. One of his big hands caressed her stomach and then moved lower to cup her sex. A gasp escaped her as his fingers grazed her clit.

He broke the kiss and smiled at her. "I need to return the favor. Slide up."

Kate had hardly scooted towards the headboard before Ric parted her legs and placed kisses to the sensitive skin of her thighs. Her breath came faster with anticipation as he neared the part of her body that ached for him.

Tasting him had turned her on like crazy and she'd grown damp while pleasuring him. She'd almost forgotten what a man tasted like and his slightly musky flavor and soft skin made her desire burn hotter. Her breath caught as he slowly stroked her with his soft, warm tongue. It was her turn to squirm as he flicked the tip of his tongue over the swollen bud within her folds.

Running her hand through his short hair, she urged him on. Kate fisted her hands in the sheets when his tongue moved faster. "Oh, God. Don't stop, please don't stop."

It was impossible to hold still as he laved and sucked. She trembled as fire flowed through her body. Everything within her became completely centered on what Ric was doing. The sensations built to a crescendo as she neared the brink. Ric's clever tongue found the exact spot that sent her over the edge.

Her voice rang off the walls as bliss took her by storm. She called his name repeatedly as he kept going, drawing her release out as long as possible. Finally, Kate flopped back on the bed, her breathing coming in pants.

"That was amazing, Ric. Oh, my God."

His laugh was low and sexy, sending shivers over her as he moved up to lie beside her. "You taste so good." Leaning over, he took her nipple in his mouth and sucked.

Kate moaned and ran her hand over his muscular shoulder. Then he released her and said, "Hang on a second. I have to get a raincoat."

She giggled at his word choice and said, "Let me get it." She pulled open her nightstand drawer and took out a condom.

*****

It wasn't the first time that a woman had put a condom on him, but there was something about the way Kate did it that drove him crazy. Maybe it was the graceful way her pretty hands moved. They were as naturally beautiful as the rest of her. Her fingers were slender yet strong and although her nails weren't very long, they were nicely shaped. She wore only clear nail polish on them and Ric found the look sexier than the manicured hands of the kind of women he usually saw.

Watching her drove him so insane that as soon as she finished, he pressed her down onto the mattress and moved between her legs as quickly as his cast would allow him to. It was a little awkward but he'd deal with it.

His eyes never left hers as he moved into her hot sheath. "You're so tight, Kate, so wet. I hope you're ready for me to fuck the shit out of you, because I can't guarantee how long I'll hold out."

Immediately, she lifted her legs and locked them around his waist. "Do your worst, cowboy."

It had been his intention to make slow, leisurely love to her, but there was something about Kate that made that impossible. He was glad that she felt the same way. She pulled him down for a hot, wet kiss as he braced his arms and started pumping his hips.

Kate moaned with each thrust, which increased in power and tempo. Ric broke into a sweat with the strain of holding back. With single-minded determination, he sought to give her as much pleasure as she could take.

The pitch of Kate's whimpers and moans rose and then she arched her back as she tightened around him. Ric thought he'd never seen anything as beautiful as Kate in that moment. The sheer delight on her beautiful face mesmerized him and his control vanished.

His climax hit him just as hers started to ebb. The intensity of it shook him, stealing his breath and making him go completely still. "Fuck, Kate. It's so good, so good..." His words trailed away into a groan as his release began fading.

Easing down on top of her, he gazed into her eyes and something inside of Ric shifted. Shoving away the crazy mix of feelings, he kissed Kate softly before rolling carefully onto his side.

"Damn, woman," he said. "You're enough to give a man a heart attack."

Kate laughed and moved to face him. "I could say the same for you. Can we have movie night again sometime?"

"Doc, we can movie night every night as far as I'm concerned. Of course, I'd prefer it without the dog bite," he said.

Kate rose into a half sitting position, looked at his arm, and winced. "Ouch. That looks nasty. How does it feel?"

"Honestly, until right now, I didn't even remember it was there," Ric said with a chuckle. "Don't worry about me, Doc. I'll be better before you know it." He ran a hand over her silky hair. "Now, how do you feel about duct tape and garbage bags?"

*****

As she looked over some blood work results on a cat the next morning, Kate had a hard time concentrating. She kept thinking about the late night shower that she and Ric had shared. When he'd brought up garbage bags and duct tape, she'd thought that he'd been talking about something kinky.

They'd laughed about it the whole time she taped the

garbage bag over his cast. Her large, walk-in shower had made bathing easy. Then they'd had a long nap before Ric had gotten up at five so he could go home to get ready to go to Denver. It had surprised her when he'd asked to stay, but pleasantly so. Sleeping in his arms felt so natural and Kate envisioned doing it a lot.

Finished looking at the results, Kate called over one of her techs named Carly. "We're going to have to start Pudding on insulin. Her blood sugars are through the roof. I'll also speak to Mr. Greer about how much he's feeding her and making sure she has fresh water every day. Her electrolytes are low, too."

Carly nodded. "Okay. I'll start getting the medication around and bring it in."

"Thanks, Carly."

Robert came over to the computer kiosk and smiled. "How was your sleepover?"

Kate was too happy to even try to pretend that she was annoyed. "Glorious. Let's just say that we could've shot our own porno."

Robert snickered. "I knew that you'd wind up in the bedroom. You look very relaxed."

Kate nodded. "So very relaxed, Robbie. Although there were many tension-filled moments last night." She nudged him with her elbow.

"I'm sure there were." He let out a wistful sigh. "I miss those kinds of moments. I really need to get laid."

"I told you that you need a girlfriend," Kate said.

Robert poked her in the ribs. "I said get laid, not get my heart stomped on again. No, I just need some straight up hot fucking."

"Robbie, you're a great looking guy. I'm sure that you can find that," she said.

He snorted. "Tried last night. Struck out."

"Aw, I'm sorry," Kate said.

"Me, too, but that's enough about me. I'll bet Ric's stressed out after this weekend, huh?" Robert asked.

"What do you mean?"

Robert's expression turned quizzical. "You don't know, do you?"

"Know what?"

"About their business problems." Robert said, "Come to my office once you're done with your next appointment."

"Okay."

Although she didn't rush through Pudding's appointment, Kate didn't dawdle, either. In a firm manner, she warned Mr. Greer that if he didn't start taking care of Pudding, that she wasn't going to be with him much longer. The middle-aged man had been contrite and promised to do right by his furry friend.

After giving some instructions to one of her other techs, Kate found Robert in his office and shut the door. "Now, what's this about Ric's business?"

Robert had an article from the Wall Street Journal pulled up on his laptop and turned it towards her so she could read it. Kate couldn't believe what she was reading.

"They're losing clients? Rumors are the firm is in financial trouble?"

"Read down further. Rumor has it the three partners are not getting along as they should and clients are bailing."

Kate met Robert's gaze. "How do you know all of this stuff?"

He shrugged. "I'm a social media junky. You know that. And I'm always interested in anything about our town. Financial trouble might mean the hospital closing since they only just bought it."

"I have to start paying more attention," Kate said as she finished the article. "No wonder Ric didn't contact me much over the weekend. Is the hospital at risk?"

Robert laughed. "Who knows? I'm not one to believe what the papers are saying but the financial pages have a bit more ethics about them."

"So why are they attracting so much attention. Perhaps a competitor wants them weakened."

"That's what I thought, but there has to be some truth to this because the investment world takes a dim view of rumors, it can ruin a firm," Robert said.

Kate said, "I'm going to text Ric around lunch and let him know I'm here if he needs someone to talk to. All that responsibility, staff, clients, the hospital, it must be a heavy burden."

Although she worried for Ric, Kate did indeed have a wonderful feeling in her soul, a lightness that she hadn't experienced in so long. It stayed with her as she treated pets and prescribed medication and she savored the good mood.

It wasn't just the phenomenal sex with Ric that made her feel that way. It was the man himself. He'd shown his kindness and understanding in the way he'd dealt with Daisy and she knew that he adored Hayley. Kate was drawn to men who loved kids and animals, which Ric did.

Talking with Ric was easy and he was so much fun to be around. All of those positive attributes combined with his insane good-looks and considerable talents in the bedroom made him the total package.

She didn't care if Ric lost every cent he had. She only cared that it would upset Ric because it was obvious he liked taking care of people. He'd feel such guilt if the hospital got into difficulties. She knew he'd worked doubly hard to ensure that did not happen.

As lunchtime neared, Kate hoped that things were going well for Ric and hoped that he'd have a few minutes to talk. She didn't examine her eagerness to hear his voice. Instead, she just enjoyed the happiness in her heart and refused to dampen it with dark thoughts of something that might never happen.

Chapter Eleven

When Ric and Tyler entered the Denver boardroom, both were apprehensive about how the meeting would play out. Chase was consumed with guilt at causing such a stir in the financial press. They hadn't talked much as they had been busy fighting the unsubstantiated rumors of impropriety. McKnight was still a client but it hadn't stopped others talking that the 'turn anything to gold' golden boys were breaking up. The market was fascinated. It was the three of them together that made Horizon Enterprises so successful and their clients wondered what would happen if that partnership imploded.

All of the other staff included in the daily meetings filed in and started getting organized.

"Doreen, any luck getting Chase?" Tyler asked.

"No. Sorry. I miss him," she said. "We sometimes cook on Sundays."

Tyler raised his eyebrows. "You cook with him?"

She nodded. "Yeah. Over Skype. We try out bizarre recipes to see if they're any good."

Ric laughed. "Sounds like Chase, all right."

The big screen on the far wall lit up and Chase appeared on it. It shocked Ric to see that he was wearing a casual blue suit.

"Morning, y'all," he said, grinning.

Everyone greeted him and Doreen waved at him excitedly. "Hi, honey!" she said. "I missed you yesterday."

"Well, hello, hot stuff. Text me what you made later on and I'll play catch-up tonight, okay?" Chase responded.

"Okay."

Ric got a kick out of the way Doreen giggled and smiled like a schoolgirl even though she was married and Chase was at least twenty years her junior. Tyler cleared his throat and gave her a pointed look, at which she sobered and fell silent.

"So, as you know, I'm an idiot and screwed up the tentative launch date for McKnight's public offer," Chase said. "I would like to formally apologize for all the inconvenience caused by my fuck-up. Villanova is completely lost to us." He looked at Ric and Tyler in turn. "I tried everything to get them to stay. I even flew to sunny Florida and played a round of golf with Big Mike on Saturday to try to smooth things over."

"You did?" Tyler asked. "Why didn't you tell us?"

Chase cocked his head. "I'm telling you now, Ty. This cluster-fuck is my fault, so I've been cleaning up after the mess I made."

The meeting members laughed and even Tyler cracked a smile over that.

"Anyway, seems like Big Mike's partner, his wife, has

him by the balls. She doesn't trust me with their business. Big Mike won't go against her wishes, happy wife means happy life. He was very regretful and promised to swing clients our way if possible," Chase said.

Ric chuckled. "Ty feels the same way about Emily. He does everything to keep her happy."

Chase laughed. "Surprising, ain't it? Now, while Big Mike isn't sticking with us, his son, Little Mike, is another matter. He's been wanting to do some investing of his own and he has a fairly impressive portfolio that he'd like to transfer over to us. Seems like he's been trying to stand on his own and feels he can use us now that his father's company isn't."

The room erupted in laughter. When things calmed down again, Tyler asked, "Did he say how soon he's coming on board?"

"Oh, I'll leave the specifics up to you guys. I'm just extending the introduction to make up for my mistake. What y'all do bores the hell out of me," Chase said. "Ric, Little Mike said he'll be in touch with you this week since he primarily lives in New York now. I gave him your number."

"Okay," Ric said.

"So what else were you up to while you were keeping us in the dark?" Tyler asked.

"Well, GQ, I just got back from a meeting with Miss Green Girl's financial gurus. I happened to serenade her when I was drowning my sorrows at a bar the other night. Seems as though she was impressed by my talent and wants to invest with us."

Doreen squealed. "I love her song, Pop Your Popper."

"I know," Chase agreed. "Catchy."

"Who the hell is Miss Green Girl?" Tyler asked.

Doreen said, "She's a new pop artist. Word is that Taylor Swift hates her because she's getting so popular now."

Chase said, "Yeah. They'll be calling you, Ty. Seems like G.G., that's what she told me to call her, likes to ski and wants you to show her the Colorado slopes this winter."

Tyler nodded. "I'd be happy to. Shoot me her number so I can sweet-talk her. She knows I'm married, right?"

Chase continued to bring them up-to-date for another half hour, at the end of which, he asked to speak to Ric and Tyler alone. Once everyone had filed from the conference room, Chase took off his suit jacket and unbuttoned his shirt.

"Look, guys, I'm sorry about screwing up like that and it won't happen again. But Ty, don't come swinging at me like that. I deserve more respect. I know how important this company is to y'all, but it's important to me, too. And believe me, I beat myself up enough for everyone after I realized what I'd done," he said.

"Yeah, I should've handled that better, Chase. Sorry about that," Tyler said. "I'm trying to learn to control this temper of mine. Permission to kick my ass when you next see me."

Ric asked, "Why did you go off the grid like that?"

Chase blew out a breath. "Because I needed to take responsibility for my actions and do whatever was necessary to fix it. I do know that as the marketing arm of this trio I'm probably very easily replaced."

Ric watch Tyler's face crumble. "Shit, Chase. I feel all kinds of terrible if that is what you think. We are closer than *brothers*. To me, and Ric, you're irreplaceable. All for one and one for all—expect where the ladies come into it, isn't that our motto."

Chase smiled sadly. "That's why I couldn't talk to you guys this weekend. Brothers can often say things they don't really mean. You needed to cool off and I needed to handle this in my own way. I was busy working on finding new blood, as you can see."

Ric chuckled. "And it doesn't hurt that some of them are in the entertainment industry. We don't have a big rep in that market. Great work, Chase."

Chase pointed at him. "Bingo. A new market for us. Loads of singers need to raise funds to make and promote their work." His expression turned grim, which alarmed Ric. "I didn't want to say anything with the others in here, but I had a call from one of Lisbon's underlings."

"Lisbon?" Tyler's expression tightened. "Why?"

Chase fidgeted. "It's my fault. They smell blood in the water and there's talk of them being interested in buying our New York office."

Ric's blood pressure rose and he pounded the table. "Like hell they will! No way are we letting those pricks take our New York business! That's my territory now and I'll be damned if they're going to move in on it."

"Don't get excited, Ric," Tyler said. "Let's keep our heads."

"That's rich coming from you," Ric retorted. "We need to call an immediate shareholders meeting and reassure the board that we're going to remain financially solvent. With the new business coming our way, it won't be a lie."

Tyler smiled at him. "Do as I say, not as I do. I'll have Drew set up the meeting and let you guys know when it is. It would be good if you could be there for it, Chase. Present a united front. Unless…Wait a second." He tapped his pen on the conference table. "What if that's what Lisbon wants. We didn't hear from any of the board members over the weekend. If we call an emergency meeting without any cause, that's going to plant doubt in their minds."

Chase rubbed his chin and yawned. "Yeah. You're right. I should've thought of that. I told Bryce that I wasn't worried and that things were fine. I guess we'll just bide our time a little and quietly feel them out."

"I think that's the right way to go about it," Ric said. "I'll send out an excited email announcing all of the new business coming our way. That way it doesn't look like we're running scared."

With their game plan in place, they adjourned the meeting and went their separate ways. Ric settled in the extra office and started composing his email. He'd just finished the rough draft of it when his text message alert went off.

Kate: Hello, my sexy dog whisperer.

He laughed at her greeting.

Ric: Hello, my gorgeous doctor.
Kate: Are you busy?
Ric: Yeah, but I can take a little break. What did you have in mind?"
Kate: Can I call you?

Ric didn't reply, instead hit the call button on the message and broke into a big smile when she answered. "Beat you to the punch, Doc."

"So you did. How are things? I heard about your business woes."

Ric was surprised by her question. "How did you hear about that?"

"Robert follows the markets as he's an investor. He saw the article in the Wall Street Journal about it and showed it to me.," she said. "There was a picture of Chase McIntyer. He's hot."

"Hey! Do I need to be jealous?" Ric asked. "You're mine."

She didn't respond right away.

"Kate? You there?"

"I'm yours? Are you getting territorial on me?"

Although there was humor in her voice, wariness was there, too. Was he getting territorial? They'd just started seeing each other and hadn't discussed being exclusive since they were supposed to be keeping things casual. But as Ric thought about it, the idea of her seeing anyone else made him jealous.

What the hell is happening here? I've been doing casual for years. What I feel for Kate isn't casual. How can that be? He thought his heart too battered from Lizzie. *We just met a couple of weeks ago. This is nuts.*

However, Ric was always honest with himself and he didn't try to brush off his feelings. He was crazy about Kate and he didn't want her dating other men. "I guess I *am* getting territorial, Kate. I didn't expect to feel that way, but I do."

"Ric, I think we should talk whenever you come back to town."

"We're not staying in Denver tonight," Ric said. "Do you

want me to come over?"

"Yeah. I should be home by seven."

"Okay. I'll see you then," he said as Tyler came into his office with a dark expression. "Take care, Doc."

"You, too."

Ric hung up and looked at Tyler.

"I just got off the phone with George Stevens," Tyler said. "It's real. Lee Lisbon called him this morning. Looks like we need to put that meeting together after all."

Ric rubbed his forehead. "I better get that email out asap. Hopefully that'll provide reassurance. What do you want to do about Lisbon?"

Tyler gave Ric his shark's tooth smile. "I have a couple of ideas. Let me run them by you."

*****

At 6:30 that night, Kate knew that she wasn't going to make it home by seven. She'd been called out to an area farm to help a cow with a breech birth and it had taken a long time to safely deliver the little Holstein calf. After spending three hours with her arm inside of a cow, she reeked of cow crap, sweat, and dirt.

There was no way that she could get home and showered in time to be ready for Ric. After the farmer thanked her again, Kate climbed tiredly into her truck and sighed before pulling out her phone and tapping Ric's icon on the screen.

"Hey, Doc."

The fatigue in his voice worried her. "Hi. Are you okay. You sound like crap."

His warm chuckle in her ear gave her goosebumps. "Gee, thanks. You sound tired, too. Bad day?"

"Not bad, just tiring. I just hauled a heifer backwards out

of a cow."

"Been there, done that. Not fun. Would you rather reschedule?"

Despite being worn out, Kate didn't cancel. "Not unless you do."

"I was hoping you'd say that."

Kate smiled. "I'm just leaving Carver's farm now, so I won't be ready until about seven-thirty. I need to shower."

"Mmm. Too bad I won't be there to wash your back."

Feeling wicked, Kate said, "I still have duct tape and garbage bags."

He laughed. "You're on. See you in a bit."

Kate had been about to protest since she'd only been teasing, but he'd already hung up. Suddenly energized by the thought of showering with Ric, Kate turned the ignition and started for home.

*****

When Kate pulled into her driveway, Ric was already there, leaning on a silver Jeep SUV. She hadn't seen him dressed up before and as he stood with one hip resting against the car in a charcoal gray suit with a white shirt and a loosened black tie, anyone would've mistaken him for a fashion model or the successful, rich and powerful investment banker that he was.

What the hell was she doing? He was way out of her league; besides, she had nothing in common with this Ric Stanford. She preferred him in sweats.

His eyes looked more silver than blue in the evening light and the stern expression on his face made him seem formidable and sexy as hell. But when he smiled at her, the warmth in the expression made him look even sexier to her.

She forgot about the powerhouse suit.

He grabbed his crutches and started towards her. "Hi. You look very pretty for someone who had her arm up a cow's crotch."

Kate laughed as she met him at the front door. "Thanks but you were standing down wind. You look fantastic. Very sharp." She took a big sniff. "And you smell good enough to eat."

The meaning of her words did not escape him as his lips broke into a smile that promised sex. "Thank you. I clean up pretty good."

The dogs met them at the door and Daisy wasn't a bit shy about greeting Ric this time. She wanted to jump on Ric and give him doggie kisses, but Kate kept her down so that she didn't knock Ric over.

"I'd say that you have a new girlfriend," Kate teased him as Daisy fawned over him.

Ric petted Daisy, keeping his bad leg well away from her. "I love you, too, Daisy. You're such a pretty girl."

He followed Kate out to the kitchen. She opened the back door and let the dogs out into the huge fenced in yard.

A loud, raucous screech made Ric jump. "What the hell was that?"

"You never got introduced to Manny, my Amazon parrot. He's letting me know that he's hungry. You want to meet him?" she asked.

"Sure."

"Fair warning: he swears. It's Phil's fault," she said, leading him into a room off the kitchen.

A huge cage stood on the far side of the room and a big, blue, green, orange, and purple parrot regally stood on a tall wooden perch.

"He's huge," Ric said. "He's gorgeous. Hi, Manny."

"Screw you," Manny said.

Kate and Ric laughed at the parrot's rude greeting.

"I guess he's not impressed with me," Ric said.

Kate started filling Manny's food dish. "Well, he's the only one. He loves attention, but he says bad things."

Manny moved closer to Kate and let out a wolf whistle. "Hey, sexy."

"Hey, handsome," she responded, petting his head.

He purred like a cat, making Ric laugh.

Kate finished feeding Manny and shut the cage door again. "Manny has an impressive repertoire. Okay. Behave. I'll come see you later."

"Later, gator," Manny agreed.

"Let me fill the dog dishes and I'll be ready to take that shower," Kate said. "In fact, why don't you start upstairs and I'll be right there?"

*****

"Sounds like a plan," Ric said, thinking that Kate looked adorable in her denim overalls, a Tweety Bird T-shirt, and a beat-up Nike ball cap.

As he made his way through the front hall to the stairs, he thought about how comfortable he felt around Kate. Maybe it was because she was so real, so genuine, or how kind she was that made him feel like he could be his true self around her.

So many of the women in his circles in New York were high-maintenance and he felt as though he was acting a part. He loved his profession and the thrill of making fantastic deals, but sometimes he just wanted to be liked for himself and not his money or influence.

While Tyler had taken to city living like a duck to water, Ric had had a little tougher time adjusting when they'd moved to the Big Apple after college. When the opportunity to open a Denver office had arisen, he'd been happy to head it up.

It meant that he would be closer to home and to Lizzie. Even though she hadn't loved him, Ric hadn't been able to shake his love for her. He knew that her misbehavior was but an act hiding a confused and lonely girl inside. One day she would settle down and he meant to be there just in case. Looking back, he realized how stupid he'd been to love a woman who only had the capacity to love herself. So much wasted time.

He shrugged off those dark thoughts as he entered the bathroom and turned on the lights. The roll of duct tape and box of garbage bags still sat on the floor by the shower. Smiling, Ric tugged his tie off and dropped it to the floor. Then he went over and sat on the straight-back chair in the corner and continued undressing.

Kate appeared just as he was unbuckling his belt and started the shower. The way she looked at him chased away his fatigue and his blood ran hotter as she started taking off her clothes. He thought she looked like a goddess as she stood naked before him, her long dark hair cascading over her shoulders.

Quickly, he shed the rest of his clothing and taped a garbage bag over his cast. They started the shower and took their time washing each other, bringing their desire to a fever pitch before becoming inventive in their hot, steamy lovemaking. Afterwards, as they stood under the shower spray holding each other, Ric knew that his desire for Kate would never be quenched.

Chapter Twelve

After scarfing down some frozen pizza and French fries, Kate and Ric settled down on the sofa with some wine. Kate put a pillow on the coffee table and had Ric prop his foot up on it. She'd put on a gray lounge outfit and a pair of slippers while Ric wore one of Phil's old robes. She should feel funny about that but she didn't. It felt right. It felt like Phil understood and liked Ric.

"Come here," Ric said, putting an arm around her shoulders.

She snuggled against his side and looked into his gorgeous eyes. "I've never been in a long distance relationship. Have you?" Putting a hand on his jaw, she stroked her thumb over his five o'clock shadow. "I don't want to stop seeing you when you go back to New York. I'm happy to earn frequent flyer miles."

His eyes widened for a moment before he smiled. "I was going to say the same thing to you." He picked up her hand

and kissed it. "I know that this was just supposed to be a casual affair, but the fact is that I'm crazy about you. You'll think I'm nuts, but I think I'm falling for you."

His statement caught Kate completely off guard. Had she heard correctly? "You are?"

He nodded. "Yeah. What do you think about that?"

Kate examined her feelings carefully. It scared her a little that she could have such strong feelings for Ric so soon, but she couldn't deny that they were there. She wasn't a schoolgirl who was crushing on a handsome boy. She knew the difference between infatuation and the kind of attraction she felt for Ric.

But was she truly ready for something more serious?

When she'd first agreed to see Ric, she'd never imagined that anything more than some companionship and sex would come of it. They led such different lives. She'd thought that it would be over when he moved back to New York. What did they have in common that could sustain a relationship, let alone a long distance one? What she shared with Phil was alive. They were both vets and loved animals. But the thought of not seeing or talking to Ric anymore depressed her.

"I feel the same way, Ric." She shook her head. "I don't understand how this could be happening, but I care for you very much. And you're not a rebound or whatever you would call that. Phil died over eighteen months ago. I still miss him, every day, but I have to live my life. What I feel is genuine."

Ric nodded. "I know Phil will always be in your heart, that's as it should be. I do hope, however, there is room for me." His words made Kate's heart skip a few beats. He tightened his embrace and lowered his lips to hers in a tender kiss that conveyed much more than physical attraction. She felt emotionally closer to him as she wound her arms around his neck and kissed him back.

When it ended, she laid her head on his chest. "Ric?"

"Yeah?"

"Would you like to stay?"

A warm chuckle sounded under her ear. "I was hoping you'd say that. I brought clothes and my shaving kit with me."

She raised her head and grinned at him. "You're pretty sure of yourself."

"No, just prepared."

"Like a boy scout, huh?"

He cocked an eyebrow at her. "I know how to tie some pretty good knots and start a fire."

"You'll have to show me that sometime," she said with a flirty look.

"Anytime you want."

A wet, cold canine nose was suddenly thrust between them.

Kate laughed and hugged Daisy's neck. "What's the matter? Are you jealous? You're going to have to get used to it. He's my boyfriend, Daisy, and I'll fight for him."

Ric squeezed her thigh and pet Daisy's back, but he caught Kate's eye. "Are you claiming me?"

Kate raised her chin a little. "Damn straight, I am."

"Good. I'm claiming you, too. No seeing other people," he said. "We can make this work, Kate. I'll come home as much as possible, although right now, I might be there a lot because we've got some problems."

The worry in his eyes made Kate concerned. "What kind of problems?"

Ric let out a heavy sigh and filled Kate in on the situation with Lisbon and Horizon's stockholders. "So I'm going to have to go to New York tomorrow to prepare for Wednesday's meeting. I should be able to come back Friday night, but I can't guarantee that."

Kate squeezed his shoulder. "It's okay. You have to take care of business. I completely understand that since I own my own practice. Do what you need to and come to me when you can."

A frown formed between his eyebrows. "Are you sure that you're going to be fine with a long-distance relationship?"

"I wouldn't say I was if I didn't mean it." His concern for her feelings was touching. "If anything it should give us time to see where this might lead."

His expression relaxed into a smile. "Do you have an objection to me leaving a toothbrush here?"

Kate looped her arms around his neck. "Not at all. In fact, you could leave a shaving kit here if you wanted too."

*****

Ric wasn't the sort of man who left his stuff at a woman's house. In fact, he rarely saw the same woman more than two or three times since he hadn't wanted to get attached. It was also why he kept hooking up with the same type of women: career women who had no desire for a husband or family.

Satisfying his physical urges and leaving when the sex was over had been a way of life for years. While he was thrown a little off kilter by Kate's offer, he was also pleased by it. He should be scared as hell over how fast things were moving between them, but he wasn't.

Kate admitted he was the first man she'd had sex with since Phil and he hoped he wasn't merely being used as a means to find her way back into the dating pool. Lizzie had been keen when they had first gotten together, then very quickly moved on. Mind you Lizzie was young, they both were.

If any other woman had suggested keeping possessions at her house, he'd have quickly said goodbye to her. However, Kate wasn't any other woman. She was different. What he loved most of all was she was the complete opposite of Lizzie. Kate was warm, fun, caring—she put others before herself. Lizzie only thought of herself, he could see that clearly now. Kate was also the sexiest woman he'd ever come across. Little by little he was talking himself into taking a chance. A big chance! To open his stuttered heart once again. For one moment he hesitated answering. She was so beautiful, sitting their hope in her eyes. However, every rose has thorns. He knew things could look rosy on the outside but underneath a wasp nest sat ready to sting. He would have to trust that Kate wasn't kidding herself, and that she had put her past behind her and was ready to move on.

"Dr. Donoghue, I would love to leave my shaving kit and toothbrush here," he said in a formal tone.

Kate's smile entranced him. "Fantastic. As much as I hate to say it, I need to hit the hay."

"Me, too. I'll go get my stuff," Ric said.

"Where are your keys? It'll be easier for me to get it, gimpy."

He scowled at her as he fished his key ring out of his pants pocket. "You're lucky you're pretty. My duffel bag is on the front passenger seat."

"Duffel bag, huh? You really are sure of yourself, aren't you?" she asked with a teasing smile.

"Hopeful, not sure," he responded.

"Yeah, yeah." She made a dismissive gesture and left Ric smiling after her.

*****

When her alarm went off the next morning, Kate was startled to feel an arm draped over her midsection. She'd missed the intimacy of these waking moments. Looking to her left, Ric's face came into focus. His jaw was slack in sleep and his rumpled hair stuck up in spots. Memories of waking up with Phil like this surfaced and she smiled..

It was one of the things she'd missed the most after Phil's death. Having someone to cuddle and share the troubles and joys of the day with. He'd been such a sweet, boyishly handsome man, who'd even been pleasant upon waking. It had irritated the crap out of her that he was so happy in the morning, but he'd always helped her start the day in a good mood.

It took barely a second to realize the pain that usually came with remembering Phil wasn't there. She loved the memories, pulled them close. They no longer strangled her in grief. She could enjoy them and look back with happiness that she'd gotten to share that wonderful man's life even if only for a few years.

She hit the snooze button and relaxed again. Ric never moved and she studied him for a little longer. His rugged handsomeness enthralled her, but his kindness and sense of humor drew her to him even more. For a highflying executive he was down to earth. His small town persona came calling as soon as he shed his designer suits. Her alarm went off again and Ric stirred this time.

"You have the second most annoying alarm clock ring," he mumbled, pulling her closer.

Kate giggled. "The second most? Who beat me out of first place?"

"Chase. He has a Sponge Bob ring on his for when he really needs to be up. Usually he has beach sounds on it that wake him up gradually."

"Would you like me to put Sponge Bob on mine?"

Ric tickled her ribs and Kate struggled to get away from him. He relented after a few moments and pressed a hard kiss to her cheek. "Good morning, Doc."

"Good morning," she said a little out of breath. "I hope you don't tickle me every morning."

"No, but there's something else I'd rather do with you every morning."

The need to pee hit Kate and she pushed at his arm. "Ric, I have to go."

"Go where?"

"The bathroom."

"Oh, sorry. I thought you were being funny," Ric said, releasing her.

Kate got up, threw a robe on, and trotted down the hall to the bathroom. Once she'd finished her business, she got in the shower. She'd just put soap on her shower sponge when Ric knocked on the bathroom door.

"It's not locked, Ric."

He poked his head inside. "I forgot to ask you if you have a downstairs bathroom."

"Yeah, why?"

"Well, I need to go."

"Oh. Just go here."

"Go here? With you in the bathroom?"

"Yeah. I mean, unless that makes you uncomfortable," she said.

"I thought women hated being in the bathroom at the same time as a guy. Emily does. Poor Ty."

Kate laughed. "I grew up with three boys and we only had one bathroom."

"You have three brothers?"

"Cousins, but we might've well have been siblings. There were times when peeing while one or the other was in the shower was unavoidable. Our bathroom was situated in a way where you couldn't see the toilet from the tub, just like in this bathroom, it's almost a separate room." Kate said. "Would it freak you out if the roles were reversed?"

"I don't know. I've honestly never gone with a woman present. Or vice versa."

Kate opened the frosted shower door and laughed at Ric's uncomfortable expression. "You're kidding? Never?"

"Never."

"Well, I've lived with a man before, so I'm used to sharing a bathroom."

"Yeah, but you and Phil were engaged. This thing with us is still new. Don't you want to retain the mystery or whatever?" Ric asked.

"Mystery? Is it really a mystery that I have to pee or anything else? I fart, too. Does that disgust you?"

Ric shook his head. "Everyone farts. I don't believe I'm discussing farting and peeing at 5:15 in the morning. Fine. If you don't care, I don't, either."

Kate went back to her shower while Ric made his way across the bathroom. "What time is your flight today?"

Silence.

Thinking that he hadn't heard her, she repeated her question. Still nothing.

"Ric? Are you okay? You didn't fall, did you?"

"No. Can you *not* talk to me?"

"Why?"

"Apparently, I have a shy bladder."

Kate almost doubled over with silent laughter and covered her mouth to muffle any sound that might escape. The toilet flushed and a moment later, she yelped when the water went ice cold.

"Oh, shit! Why did you do that?" she demanded smacking the showerhead so it faced away from her.

"Sorry! Again: not used to sharing a bathroom."

The water had just warmed up when it went cold again. "What are you doing?"

"Washing my hands!"

"Oh, okay. How about you just warn me next time so that I can be prepared. I have nothing against cold showers, I just like to be forewarned," she said, popping her head out of the shower again.

His chagrined expression as he came over and sat down on the straight-backed chair was priceless. "This bathroom stuff is going to take a little getting used to, I think."

Kate said, "Ric, I'm a vet. I spend most of my life knee deep, or arm deep, in crap and other animal body fluids. To me this is a natural part of living. I know that just because I might not be shy about stuff like that, other people are. No biggie. Do whatever makes you comfortable. There is another bathroom attached to master bedroom. I moved out of that room when Phil died. Too many memories."

"Okay. To answer your question, we have a 10 a.m. flight." He taped a bag over his leg and hopped over to the shower.

He'd just shut the shower door when there was a noise at the bathroom door.

"What was that?" he asked.

"Cinders. I usually leave the bathroom door open since it's just me. They like to keep me company while I'm getting around."

Actual knocking sounded on the bathroom door then.

"That's no dog," Ric said.

"Hey, Special K! You going running or what?"

Her eyes rounded when she recognized Robert's voice. "Oh, no! I forgot that I was going running with Robert. Damn." Her face turned scarlet at Ric's incredulous look. "Um, no, not this morning. I forgot to call you last night to tell you. Sorry!"

"Let me guess. You have company this morning."

"Yes. Now, get out of here. I'll see you at work."

"Hi, Ric! Nice to meet you, so to speak," Robert said.

Ric glared at the door. "Yeah. You, too."

His hard tone said that it was anything but nice to be talking to Robert right then.

"Now, now, Ric. You're going to have to get used to the fact that Kate's best friend is a man."

"Robert!" Kate shouted, mortified that Robert was getting cocky at that particular moment. "I'll see you at work!"

"Okay. Later!"

Ric pointed at the bathroom door, his eyes blazing with

anger. "Does he come in your house like that all the time?"

Kate defiantly put her hands on her hips. One slipped off because of her slick skin and she had to put it back. "Yes. He's my best friend and he has a key to the house. He didn't know that you were going to be here this morning."

"No, but he had to have seen my car. He knew damn well that I was here and he came in anyway just to make a point to me," Ric said. "Are you sure that he doesn't have feelings for you?"

Kate tried not to laugh, but couldn't quite manage it. "Trust me, Robert is not interested in me. We met on a blind date and when it was over, he said, 'Kate, you're a beautiful, wonderful woman, but there is just no spark here.' We've been best friends ever since." She put a hand on Ric's shoulder. "If this is going to work, we're going to have to trust each other. I trust you. Do you trust me?"

Ric put an arm around her. "Yes, I do." He chuckled. "I guess I'm the jealous type. It is strange that your best friend is a guy. I'll adjust. But if he makes a wrong move towards you, I'm going to beat the shit out of him. I'm just giving you fair warning."

Kate thought his jealousy was sweet, but she didn't want there to be any problem between the two men. That kind of tension wasn't good for a relationship of any kind.

"Okay, caveman. You warned me, but I promise you that Robert doesn't have any romantic feelings for me. Phil and him were very close. Give Robert a chance and you'll become good friends, too," she said.

"You're right," Ric said. "I'll play nice."

Kate kissed him. "Thank you." She sighed as she caressed his chest a little. "I have to get going, but call me when you land in New York so I know you made it safely, okay?"

"I will. I'll call you tonight, too," he said, hugging her close.

"You better."

He bit her earlobe. "Sure you can't stay just a little longer?"

She shuddered as desire spread through her, but she pushed away from him. "I'd love to, but I have several surgeries today and I don't want to get behind."

He gave her an understanding smile. "Go on then. Go save the animal kingdom."

Kate laughed as she exited the shower. "Just lock up before you go."

"Okay, Doc."

When Kate opened the bathroom door, the dogs came in and the scent of fresh coffee hit her. "Hey, Ric. Robert made coffee before he left."

"That was nice of him. I could use some. I'm not a morning person, so caffeine in the morning is a necessity."

Kate finished drying off. "Same here. Okay. I'll see you later."

"Bye, honey."

As she dressed, Kate listened to Ric talk to the dogs as he showered. Cinders yipped a couple of times and Rocco "talked" to him in moaning whines. It was so nice to have a man in the house again, but that wasn't the reason she wanted to keep seeing Ric. She wasn't one of those women who had to have a man around because she was afraid to be alone.

Kate had always been independent, even when her and Phil had been together, and she wasn't about to give up her self-sufficiency for Ric. That's why it was important for him to understand that she wasn't going to ditch Robert for him.

Going downstairs, she found that Robert had filled the dog dishes in addition to making coffee. She found a note on the notepad that she left on the counter that read, "I like him."

She smiled as she filled her travel mug with coffee and gathered up her backpack. She hurried out to her truck and got underway. As she drove to work, happiness flooded her soul and she thanked God for bringing Ric Stanford into her life.

Chapter Thirteen

Late that afternoon, Ric and Tyler were seated in Ric's office, brainstorming and looking over their presentation for the following day for errors. Their team had also worked on it and they felt that what they'd come up with would reassure and inspire their board and stockholders.

Tyler sighed and closed his laptop. "I think that about covers it. I could use a drink."

Ric finished making a couple of notes and nodded. "Yeah. Sounds good. Where do you want to go?"

"How about Farley's place. I don't know about you, but I don't want to run into a bunch of people we know and have to talk shop. I think a good break tonight would be good for us. Beer, sports, and junk food," Tyler said. "How does that sound to you?"

"Excellent."

Ric's Skype notification on his laptop went off. "It's Chase."

Tyler rolled his chair around so that he could see, too.

Ric hit the answer button and Chase came into view. A jolt of shock ran through Ric when he saw tears rolling down Chase's cheeks.

"Chase? What's wrong?"

Agony was etched on Chase's face and his brown eyes were red-rimmed and puffy. He put a hand to his chest and inhaled sharply. "It's Smiley," he said in a tremulous voice. "I just got word when I landed that he was…" He broke down for a few moments. "He was in a car wreck when he went out to get lunch. Oh, God. He didn't make it."

Ric and Tyler were rendered mute by the horrible news. Chase went out of sight, but they heard his harsh sobs and the floor of what looked like a restroom floor. Ric knew that outside of him and Tyler, Bruce was Chase's best friend.

Tyler cleared his throat as he blinked away tears. "Chase, where are you?"

Chase came back into view, wiping his eyes with toilet paper. "I'm still at the airport. I just booked the first flight they have back to L.A. I have to get to the hospital and start making funeral arrangements since he didn't have anyone. He was the first friendly face when I came to LA and I owe him."

"Buddy, are you all right to fly by yourself? Do you want one of us to go with you?"

Chase shook his head. "No, you gotta take care of things there. I'm sorry you have to do it without me, but doing right by Smiley is more important to me than stockholders right now. I'll be okay. I gotta pull it together for my crew, you know? They're all just as torn up as me."

Ric brushed away tears. "Us, too. He was a good friend

and an asset to our firm. Do whatever you need to do. We're all going to miss him. Call us later when you have more information, okay? Doesn't matter what time it is. Don't worry about us."

Chase took a deep breath and nodded. "Yeah. Thanks, guys. Okay. Talk to you later."

They hung up with Chase and looked at each other.

"I can't believe it," Tyler said, rubbing his temple. "I'm going to miss Smiley like hell."

Ric smiled even though his throat ached from grief. "Yeah. He used to rag on me about Junior being my favorite driver. He made a hell of a cheeseburger, too."

Tyler stood up. "Let's go tell the others. It should come from us. The news might've already spread, though."

Ric nodded and followed Tyler, dreading having to inform their employees about such a tragic loss.

*****

Ric didn't make it back to Cooper's Creek for two weeks because he was kept busy putting out one fire after another. Their stockholders' meeting had been successful, but in the wake of Smiley's death, it hadn't been as satisfying as it normally would've been.

Other issues had cropped up, requiring Ric's full attention, too. He and Kate talked at night and Ric was grateful to her for listening to him. He returned the favor, commiserating with her when she'd had to put a horse and two dogs down in one week. It frustrated him that he couldn't be there to hold her, but there wasn't anything he could do about it.

Both of them had their separate responsibilities, so they had to put their personal wants and desires on hold for the time being. On the night before he was supposed to fly to Denver, Ric prayed that nothing came up to keep him in New York. His need to see Kate was overwhelming and he couldn't wait to get home.

He admitted to himself that his feelings for Kate had intensified even more since he'd been gone. The intense desire he felt for her was a part of it, but more importantly, he missed sitting and talking with her. Communicating over phone and Skype was all right, but he needed to be with her in person.

Sitting in the living room of the apartment that used to belong to Tyler, Ric suddenly found the place too big and empty for just one person to occupy after having lived with Tyler and Emily for almost a month. He missed Hayley like crazy and talked to her every day, too.

Since nothing on TV interested him, Ric decided to go to bed. As he undressed, he thought once again about how nice sleeping with Kate in his arms had been. That simple closeness was addicting and Ric craved Kate in more way than one when he got in bed that night. He tried to relax and drift off, but he was wide awake.

Picking up his phone, he saw that it was 11:30, which meant that it was only 9:30 in Cooper's Creek. Hopefully, he could catch Kate before she went to bed. He hit her icon and waited for her to pick up.

"Hey, cowboy."

Ric grinned like an idiot when he heard her voice. "Hi, Doc. Were you sleeping?"

"No. I'm just sitting in bed reading veterinary medical journal articles. Your dog is on the bed with her head on the pillow you slept on," Kate said.

"*My* dog?"

"Mmm hmm. Daisy has been moping the whole time you've been gone. She imprinted on you, so she's your dog now. Every night she sleeps with that pillow."

That concerned Ric. "I can't take her, Kate. I'd hate to see her cooped up in the apartment all day. I'd have to hire someone to take her out and everything."

"I didn't mean for you to take her. I just meant that whenever you're here, she's yours."

Ric hadn't had a dog since he'd been a kid and he loved the idea of having one again, even if it was only part-time. "Okay. I accept."

Kate chuckled in his ear. "I guess I have to get used to sharing you a little."

"Don't feel bad. I have to share you with Cinders, so I guess we're even."

He heard Kate muffle a yawn. "Sounds like you're beat. Go to sleep, honey."

"I don't want to. I want to talk to you. Do you want to hear something crazy?"

"Of course."

Kate's voice took on a shy note. "I miss sleeping with you. I know you only stayed here a couple of times, but I really liked having you here."

Her admission warmed Ric's heart. "I feel the same way. I have an idea. Why don't we both get comfy and we'll leave our phones on and fall asleep together?"

Kate giggled and in his mind, Ric saw the way her eyes sparkled when she laughed. "I love that idea."

Rolling over on his side, Ric hit the speaker button and laid his phone on the nightstand. "Can you hear me?"

"Loud and clear."

"Good."

They chit-chatted a little longer before Ric heard Kate snore softly. Smiling, he drifted off, his slumber restful for the first time since he'd been back in New York.

*****

Kate was in the middle of sending an email to a pharmaceutical rep who'd told her that he could get her anesthesia at a cheaper price than she was currently paying when she heard a knock on the doorjamb of her office door. Looking up, she was surprised to see Ric standing there looking yummy in jeans and a Hunter green Polo shirt.

Somehow, Kate kept from squealing like a school girl, but she did rush out of her chair and into his arms. Eagerly, she met his lips and the flame between them was instantly ignited. Ric closed the office door and pinned her against it as their kiss turned hungry.

Kate ran her hands over his broad chest and wanted to rip his clothes off. She wanted him to sweep everything off her desk and make love to her on it. Reluctantly, she broke their kiss and grinned at him.

"You are a sight for sore eyes," she said. "I missed you so much."

"I missed you, too. Notice anything different about me?"

Kate looked him over and then saw the walking boot on his leg. "No more cast or crutches!"

"Nope. I just have to wear this for a couple of weeks and do some PT and I'll be as good as new. It feels so good to be out of that cast."

Kate hugged him tightly. "I'm so happy for you. No more garbage bags and duct tape."

Ric laughed. "That's right. I'm glad to be walking instead of hopping around. Emily wanted me to invite you to dinner at their house tonight. Is that okay? I don't want you to feel pressured about it."

Kate was happy that Emily and Tyler liked her. "That's fine with me. They can tell me embarrassing stories from when you guys were kids."

He rolled his eyes. "Crap. Maybe I'd better rethink this plan."

"Oh, no. We're going and that's that, buddy."

Ric groaned and kissed her again. "Okay. Might as well get it over with."

"I have something for you," Kate said.

"I have something for you, too," Ric said, rubbing his hips against her.

Kate laughed when she felt his hard-on against her stomach. "Believe me, I want that, but you'll have to wait until tonight."

"But what am I supposed to do with it in the meantime?"

Kate said, "Well, cowboy, you might have to take things in hand for the moment." The image of Ric performing self-gratification turned her on even more than she already was.

Ric smiled and moved away from her a little. "Nah. I can wait, but just be prepared for a long night."

Kate grinned as she stepped over to her desk and took a small box from her desk drawer. "Here you go."

Ric took it and gave her a quizzical look before opening it. He lifted out a house-key on an Earnhardt keychain.

"Now you have your own key to my house," she said.

Ric stared at it for a moment and then at her. "Are you sure? This is a big step, Kate."

Kate's nerves jangled as she looked into his eyes. "I know, and I won't pretend that I'm not scared somewhat, but it just feels right. Everything about you feels right. Does that make sense?"

"Yeah. It makes complete sense," he said. "I feel the same way about you."

Someone knocked on the door, making them jump. The interruption frustrated Kate, but she tamped down her irritation and opened the door.

Robert stood on the other side, clipboard in hand. He went to say something and then caught sight of Ric. "Oops. Sorry. I didn't know you had company."

"It's okay. I'm glad that you guys can formally meet now," Kate said. "Robert Chambers, this is Ric Stanford."

*****

As Ric held out a hand to Robert and smiled, he took the other man's measure. Robert wasn't quite as tall as Ric, but he was muscular and good-looking. He saw that Robert was sizing him up, too.

"Good to meet you, Ric," Robert said, shaking his hand. "Sorry for being a smart ass a couple of weeks ago, but I just can't help myself sometimes."

Ric said, "No harm, no foul. Nice to meet you, too. I'm looking forward to getting to know Kate's best buddy."

Ric watched Robert closely for any trace of jealously, but he found none in Robert's friendly expression.

"Same here," Robert said.

Ric said, "Well, Doc, I'll let you get back at it, but I'll see you at Emily's. Just come over whenever you're done tonight." He turned to Robert. "In fact, if you don't have any plans, why don't you come to dinner, too, Robert?"

"Oh, I couldn't. I wouldn't want to impose," Robert said, shaking his head.

"You're not. I'm inviting you," Ric assured him. "I hope you guys like barbequed chicken."

"Love it," Kate said.

Robert gave Kate an uncertain look, obviously concerned that she'd be angry if he accepted Ric's invitation.

"Robert, I insist that you come tonight," he said. "Glad that's settled." He kissed Kate's cheek. "See you guys tonight."

He smiled to himself over their surprised expressions as he left Kate's office. When he got into his rental car, he put the key that Kate had given him on his keyring. Happier than he'd ever been, he set out for home to see if there was anything he could do to help Emily with supper.

Chapter Fourteen

The meal that night turned into something of a party since Emily's best friend, Brooke, and Tucker also came over. It was noisy and lively and Kate had a blast. She'd missed the kind of fun chaos a large family brings to a meal and the group assembled at the Jeffries house brought back memories of her upbringing.

Hayley was a constant source of amusement with her bubbly personality and the funny remarks she made about things.

Tucker had been talking about flat tires when she chimed in with, "I don't know why they don't make tires out of something better than air."

Tucker smiled. "What would you recommend, Miss Hayley?"

She narrowed her blue eyes as she thought hard. "Sponges inside the rubber."

"Interesting. Why sponges?" Ric inquired, his eyes

twinkling.

"Well, they'd still be soft so the car rode nice, but if you run over a nail, the tire won't go flat. See? Problem solved," she said with an emphatic nod.

Kate laughed along with the rest. She'd watched Ric with Hayley and saw the close bond they shared. *He's a natural-born father. I can't believe that he's not married with a bunch of kids by now. He obviously loves them.* In her mind's eye, she conjured the image of the two of them with several children.

Then she chided herself for getting carried away with that kind of thinking. Their relationship was much too new to be daydreaming about marriage. They'd just entered the girlfriend/boyfriend phase. And while she couldn't ignore what her heart was telling her, they were a long way from exchanging nuptials.

To distract herself from her thoughts, she asked Emily if she could have the recipe for the chicken coating and started discussing cooking in general. When the meal was over, she offered to help clean up, but Emily assured her that she and Brooke had everything under control, so she went to the dining room where an impromptu card game was being set up.

*****

Ric had taken Coco outside to stretch his ankle a little. When he came back in the kitchen door, Emily waylaid him.

"So things seem to be going very well with Kate," she remarked.

He couldn't deny that. "Yeah, they are."

"How well?"

Ric could've put her off about it, but he didn't want to.

He actually welcomed her opinion. "Maybe too well."

Emily stopped loading the dishwasher to look at him. "What do you mean?"

Ric moved closer and lowered his voice. "She's the most amazing woman I've ever met. I haven't felt this way about a woman since Lizzie."

Emily's face lit up and she grabbed his arm excitedly. "I liked Kate from the first moment I met her. I think you guys are perfect for each other."

Ric laughed a little self-consciously. "I can't disagree with you there. But isn't it too soon? I mean, we only met a month ago. I don't want to rush things."

Emily leaned a hip against the counter. "Does she feel that things are moving too fast?"

"No. In fact, she just gave me a key to her house. I'll be staying there a lot."

"That's awesome," Emily said. "Look, both of you are adults and if you make each other happy, who's to tell you what's too fast and what's not? As long as it feels right to you and Kate, that's all that matters."

"It's the craziest thing. I kept running from a real relationship because it wasn't the right time. Our business was too important for me to get tied down with someone. But maybe Lizzie hurt me more than I could admit. Then I meet Kate and we just clicked. She lost a fiancé, a man she shared a home and who she was going to build a life with. If she's willing to give me a chance I'd be silly not to. She's agreed to have a long-distanced relationship and is understanding when things come up," he said. "She's gorgeous and smart and fun—everything a man could want. I think I could fall in love with her."

Emily embraced him tightly. "I'm so happy for you! I've been hoping that you would meet someone special and I think Kate is a very special woman."

Ric hugged her back as his heart flooded with happiness. "So do I. I'm glad that you approve."

"I definitely approve and if you let her get away, I'll never let you live it down."

"I won't. I intend to keep her."

"Good."

Ric gave her a last squeeze and released her. "Do you want me to help you finish up? I thought Brooke was helping you."

Emily giggled. "I think she got caught up talking to Robert. I noticed some flirty looks between them during dinner."

"Really?" That pleased Ric no end. "Great. I guess his girlfriend recently dumped him. Maybe Brooke and him will hit it off."

"Could be," Emily said. "Now, go be with your girlfriend. I'm almost done here."

"Okay. Don't take too long or Ty will come looking for you," Ric said and joined the loud group in the dining room.

*****

Later that night as Kate lay draped over Ric, catching her breath from a rowdy round of lovemaking, a feeling of such contentment stole over her. The evening at Emily and Tyler's house had been one of the most fun she'd had in quite a while. It made her feel good that his family and friends liked her, too.

He ran his hands over her back. "Whatcha thinking about, Doc?"

"You. Me. Us."

"What about you, me, and us?"

"You make me so happy, Ric." She raised her head and met his heavy-lidded, sated gaze. "I haven't been happy in a while."

Something in her expression must have tipped him off that she wanted to have a serious conversation because, with her still on top of him, he pulled himself up into a sitting position against the headboard. But when she made a move to get off him, he pressed her hips down.

"Stay there, honey," he said. "What's on your mind?"

Running her hands over his muscular shoulders, Kate gathered her thoughts. "I've always been a risk-taker, even as a little kid. While other girls were playing Barbies and having tea parties, I was outside with my cousins building ramps and jumping my bike over them. And not some girly bike, either. BMX all the way."

Ric smiled. "I can believe that about you. I'd have loved to have played with you."

"I'm sure you would have. I've always craved that adrenaline rush from defying the odds and winning," Kate said. "I push myself to the limit, past any fear I feel, and never let something defeat me. Phil and I were alike that way. God, how I loved him and when he died, I was crushed. We were partners in every way. Our practice, our interests—everything.

"I know you're a little jealous of Robert, but you don't need to be. If it wasn't for him, I'm not sure what would've happened to me. He got me through the worst, darkest period of my life and helped me see that I still had a lot to live for."

Ric squeezed her thighs lightly. "I'm glad you had him to

count on. No one should be alone during a time like that."

"Me, too. He saw me at my weakest and helped me put the pieces of my life back together," Kate said. "I was determined to keep my heart locked up. The pain of loss is indescribable to someone who hasn't suffered it. I couldn't go through that again, I can't go through that again, but then I met you and all my fear evaporated.

"You make me feel alive, something I haven't truly felt since Phil died. I'm ready to take that risk again. I'm ready to open my heart again and let it fly." She cupped his face and stared intently into his eyes. "I love you, Ric."

*****

Ric's heart thudded in his chest as he absorbed her words. Half of him was filled with joy while the other half was certain that he'd misheard her. "You what?" he croaked.

Kate smiled. "I love you. I've fallen in love with you."

He looked at her suspiciously. "Where you eavesdropping on me and Emily tonight?"

"What? No! Why would you ask me that?"

Ric looped his arms around her waist. "Because we were discussing this very topic."

She arched a pretty eyebrow at him. "You were?"

"We were. I told her that you're an incredible woman and that I've never met anyone like you. I've been running from love for a long time, ever since Lizzie died, but I'm done running, Kate. You make me happier than I've ever been and I'm so glad that you love me, because I love you, too," he said.

Tears welled in her eyes. "Please don't just say that because I said it to you, Ric. I wasn't trying to get you to say it, I just wanted you to know how I feel."

Ric leaned forward, embracing her tighter. "I'll never lie to you, Kate, especially not about something so important. I mean every word: I love you."

"Are you sure?"

"Positive."

Her smile took his breath away as she threw her arms around neck and hugged him close. "I love you, Ric."

He closed his eyes as tears burned in them. To hear those words from her was more moving than anything he'd ever felt and he couldn't help his strong reaction. "I love you, too, Kate."

When she drew back, he brushed away a couple of tears from her face and she did the same for him. They laughed together and exchanged a tender kiss that conveyed their newfound feelings to each other. As the kiss deepened, Ric's desire for Kate flared again and he rolled over with her.

Ric didn't say it again as they became wrapped up in each other, but he showed her in every other way how much he loved her. He gave her as much pleasure as he possibly could, making every move, each kiss, and caress count. Powerful emotion filled him as he felt his love returned to him as they reached the summit together.

Looking in her beautiful eyes while they remained in each other's arms afterwards, Ric knew that he'd finally found the woman of his dreams. Kate was the woman he'd been waiting for all of his life and he planned to never let her go.

*****

On Sunday of the following weekend, Kate groaned as she rolled over in bed. Her and Robert had gone hiking to Lost Falls in Rocky Mountain National Park yesterday and the demanding hike had shown her that she was a little out of shape.

"What's the matter?" Ric asked, yawning.

"That hike kicked my ass. It's been a long time since I went on a really hard hike like that. I should've listened to Robbie. He said that we should do an easier hike, but did I listen? Oh, no. I had to—oh!"

She broke off as she felt Ric straddle her legs. His large, capable hands settled on her shoulders and started massaging her sore muscles.

"I'll give you a million dollars if you don't stop," she mumbled against her pillow.

"Our sex marathon last night probably didn't help any," Ric said, chuckling.

Kate grinned. "Probably not, but at the time, I wasn't feeling any pain. Of course, I'd had a couple of glasses of wine, so that might be why."

She groaned and moaned as Ric gave her a full-body massage, even working on her feet and toes.

When he finished, he said, "Stay right there. I'll go let the dogs out."

"Okay. I wasn't planning on moving anyway. I feel like Jello now. I don't think I can walk."

Ric called the dogs to him and Kate listened to them troop down the stairs after him. A few minutes later, she heard the bathtub running. Ric's bad humming made her smile. His phone went off.

"Hey, answer me! Chase is calling you!"

Kate roused and crawled over to it. Normally, she wouldn't touch Ric's phone, but she wanted to talk to Chase and she didn't have his number. She tapped the answer button.

"Hello," she said in a throaty purr. "Is this Chase McIntyre, the hottest man in LA?"

"Why, yes, it is. This must be the luscious Dr. Donoghue," he responded. "I take it that Rikki-Tikki-Tavi isn't close at hand."

"No, but he has great hands. He just gave me a massage and I think he's drawing me a bath."

Chase laughed. "That was awful nice of him. Are you planning on thanking him?"

"Oh, I thanked him for a long, long time last night. I prepaid," she said, giggling.

"Then he definitely owed you. Glad he's paying back his debt."

Kate chuckled and got out of bed. "I'll hand you off to Ric, but it was nice talking to you, Chase."

"You, too, darlin'. Hit me up on Skype sometime. My ID is chasethedream."

"Sure it is," she laughed. "I might do that sometime."

Ric looked over at her from where he stood by the sink. She held his phone out to him. "Chase would like to speak with you, Rikki-Tikki-Tavi."

He frowned as he took the phone. "Thanks. You just had to tell her, didn't you?"

"You even put bath salts in it for me. Chase, he's a keeper," she said loudly.

Ric grinned as she slipped into the tub and sank into the hot water with a sigh of contentment. Closing her eyes, Kate relaxed, only half-listening to Ric. Her muscles loosened even further as the bath salts seeped into her pores.

"Kate, lift your head."

She opened her eyes and did as he asked, smiling when he placed a folded towel behind her head for her to rest it on. "You're so sweet."

"None of your business," Ric said into his phone even as he winked at Kate. "Hold on, Chase. Elaine is on the other line. I'll call you back later on. Yeah. Okay."

Kate enjoyed watching Ric no matter what he was doing. She thought that he was a beautiful man with all those muscles, sandy blond hair and chiseled jaw. Just looking at him gave her pleasure.

"Elaine? You're calling me on a Sunday. You never call me on a Sunday."

Kate felt a stab of concern at the way heat crept up Ric's neck into his face.

"Those rotten bastards! Does Tyler know? Don't worry about it. I'll call him and Chase. You start calling the board members," Ric said. "I'll book a flight right away."

He hung up and paced back and forth.

"What's wrong?" Kate asked.

"It's those Lisbon pricks. They're starting up their bullshit again, going after our stockholders. We're they're biggest competition in New York and they want to buy us out," Ric said. "If they rattle enough investors, they could end up owning 49% which would make our lives hell."

"You three would still have control at 51% though?"

"Yes, but with partners who we might not want to work with. It would change everything." He came over and knelt by the tub. "I'm so sorry, honey. You know that I wasn't planning on going back until Monday night, but I don't have a choice."

The dismay and anger in his gaze made Kate's heart flood

with sympathy. "I know that you wouldn't go if it wasn't so important. I'm disappointed, but I understand."

"I wish you could go with me," he said.

"Me, too. But even if I did, you'd still be working and I'd be all alone," she said.

"Yeah." He let out a growl of frustration and rose. "I have to call Ty and Chase."

Kate rose and got out of the tub. She dried off quickly and followed Ric into her bedroom to dress. Once she'd pulled on jeans and a sweatshirt, she went downstairs and started making omelets after she let the dogs in.

Ric came striding into the kitchen in jeans and a white dress shirt. He looked sexy as hell as he sat down at the table and put on his sneakers. His ankle was coming along and he'd stopped wearing the walking boot. There was still a slight hitch in his gait, that physiotherapy was helping, but otherwise, he was fine.

She set a plate and a cup of coffee down in front of him. "Eat. Doctor's orders."

He smiled at her. "Yes, ma'am."

She rubbed his shoulder briefly and went back to the stove.

"My flight leaves at eleven," he said between bites. "So I gotta get on the road."

Kate filled a travel mug with coffee, added cream to it, and set it on the table. "For the drive. To keep you awake."

He finished his omelet in three more bites. "You're too good to me. You should've enjoyed your bath longer."

"It was a very nice bath. Between that and the massage you gave me, Rikki-Tikki-Tavi, I feel much better," she said.

Although she knew how serious the situation with

Horizon's stockholders was, she hated that Ric was leaving again. She missed him already.

"I'm glad." He polished off his coffee and brought his plates over to the sink. "I'm sorry that I couldn't at least eat with you."

"Stop apologizing," Kate said, following him to the front door.

He said goodbye to the dogs and then took her in his arms. "I'll call you when we get to the apartment. I love you."

Kate's heart swelled every time he said it to her. "I love you, too. Be careful."

"I will."

He gave her a long, toe-curl worthy kiss before going out the door. Kate sighed as she closed it and then brightened. Picking up her phone, she called Emily. They commiserated for a few moments and then made plans to go for lunch and mani-pedis.

Humming, she went back upstairs to change into something nicer to wear to a girls' day out. Although she'd been looking forward to spending the day with Ric, Kate wasn't going to sit around and mope because he'd left. Once she'd dressed, Kate grabbed her keys and headed into town to run a couple of errands before meeting Emily and Hayley.

Chapter Fifteen

After a bitch of a week, Ric had arrived back in Colorado and was just picking up his luggage at Denver International when his phone rang. He saw that it was Robert and answered.

"Hey, Robert," he said. "What's up?"

"Where are you?"

"At the airport. I just got off the plane. Why?" The back of Ric's neck prickled with warning.

"Kate's in the ER."

"What happened?" Ric started jogging through the airport to the parking garage. His ankle hurt, but he didn't give a shit.

"We went rock climbing this morning with the mountain rescue team and the lead line frayed and broke. I was able to catch her and stabilize her, but her back smacked the rock face we were climbing up," Robert said.

"What do you mean the rock you were climbing with the mountain rescue team?"

"We are part of the volunteer rescue unit. We practice. Didn't you know? Look, let's save this chat for later. She needs you."

Ric swallowed his fear. "How bad is she hurt?" Ric gained the exit and sprinted for his car.

"I'm not sure, she's in radiology right now."

"I'm on my way. Just getting in my car now. Call if you have any news."

Ric threw his suitcase in the car and got in the driver's seat. "Thanks, Robert."

Ric hung up and took a few moments to calm himself so he could drive. Then he drove out of the parking garage and got on the exit ramp for the highway. As he sped along, his blood pounded through his veins as he fought back panic.

His mind went back in time to the night when he'd gotten the call from Tyler that Lizzie was missing. He remembered accompanying Ty and finding the car accident. Both Simon and Lizzie had been high on drugs and booze and had been racing another car. Simon had hit ice and lost control, wrapping the car around a tree. Lizzie hadn't been wearing a seatbelt and she'd been thrown from the car. The bastards they'd been racing, simply drove away and left them. It was snowing and the snow broke her fall. But with a broken pelvis and leg she'd lain there unable to move and had actually frozen to death while Simon lay comatose in the car not more than twenty feet away.

Ric had been the one to find her. She'd looked so serene, as if in death she had finally found peace. He would never forget how still she was, and how stiff from the cold.

Ric's heart had been ripped apart, left in tattered shreds that had taken a long time to heal. He blamed himself. This was the woman he loved yet, he'd given up on her. He'd known Simon was no good for her and yet he'd put his pride first instead of trying harder. He should have confided in Ty, let him know about the drugs. He just didn't know how to talk to a woman who thought risk was the word for fun.

Although his heart had mended, the scars of that pain had remained. Until Kate had come along, that was. She'd shown him that loving someone didn't mean 'until something more exciting came along'. A love based on respect and putting another's feelings before your own could be empowering and uplifting.

During the time that he'd been gone, his feelings for Kate had intensified. They'd talked every night and had even fallen asleep together over the phone several times. Although they'd spoken briefly about all of the things about their respective professions that were stressing them, they'd mostly told each other more about their lives and gotten to know each other better.

However, he hadn't asked more about her rock climbing and other sports. How could he love a woman he barely knew, he didn't even know she was on a volunteer rescue team. *Don't you usually ask about that sort of stuff? Why didn't I? Mountain rescue in Coopers Creek was a necessity. He'd never had a desire to climb, roping and football were his loves. Why did it have to be her that risked life and limb climbing?*

And now, the woman he loved with all his heart was severely hurt. For what? *You know why—she wants to help people. But who keeps her safe?* It seemed so risky to Ric, and reminded him of Lizzie, the thrill before all else, no matter who was worrying about you. He tried to put that out of his mind and keep his attention on the road.

When he was about twenty minutes away from Cooper's Creek, Ric called Robert, but there was still no news. Ric thanked him, hung up, and pounded on the steering wheel a few times while a string of profanity spewed forth from him.

Since he'd vented a little of his frustration, Ric felt slightly better as he pulled into the Cooper's Creek Medical Center parking lot. He found the nearest parking spot, ran through the ER entrance, and spotted Robert in the waiting room. He sat talking quietly to Emily, who saw him.

She came to him, embracing him tightly. "We're hoping that the doctor will be out shortly."

Ric hugged her back and released her. "What the hell happened?" he asked Robert as they shook hands.

"A defective lead line. It started unraveling and wouldn't hold her weight." Robert thrust a hand through his dark hair. "We checked over every piece of equipment before we left the house, just like we always do, and it looked fine. No cuts, no frayed places, nothing. We were about forty feet up when it started unraveling."

"Forty feet? In the air?" Ric practically yelled.

"Ric! Shh!" Emily admonished him.

Robert continued. "As soon as she noticed it, Kate told me and I started hauling ass to catch up to her. I was almost there when the line snapped and she fell. She was hooked to me, of course, but I wasn't sure if my little nut was going to hold since it was such a small crack."

Completely unfamiliar with those terms, Ric shook his head. "What?"

"The equipment that goes in a crack in the rock face is called a nut. It's like an anchor." Robert let out a frustrated breath. "Anyway, I grabbed the end of the remaining line that was still attached to her and between that and my anchoring, I was able to keep her from falling further. But she swung and hit the rock face hard. Her back took the brunt of the impact."

Ric put a hand over his mouth for a moment, trying to get a grip on his anger and fear. "How did you get down?"

Robert shook his head, a mystified expression on his face. "You'll think I'm crazy, but I swear that Phil was with us. I secured her to my harness and started down. Phil was the best climber I've ever seen. He could find hand and footholds when no one else could.

"I tried not to panic and all at once, I heard Phil, just as plain as day, say, 'Easy does it, Robbie. See that hold over to your right? Start there.' And I'll be damned, but it was right there."

A chill ran down Ric's spine. He'd had a few strange experiences of his own after his mother's death and he believed in spirits. "Maybe he was," he said softly. "It wouldn't surprise me. I'd come back from the dead to save Kate, too."

Robert gave a shiver. "Little by little, we got down to the bottom and then I called for help. The cell reception sucked, but I was able to make the 911 operator understand where we were."

"Thank God," Ric said.

"Yeah."

Ric noticed the bandage on Robert's left hand for the first time. "You okay?"

Robert lifted his hand. "Yeah. Bad rope burn and some scrapes, but I'll be fine."

Impulsively, Ric hugged him. "Glad to hear it. Thank you for saving her."

"She's my best friend. No way in hell was I going to let her fall," Robert said.

Ric nodded as Emily led them over to the chairs. They sat down, just as a nurse came out and asked for Kate's family.

Robert patted Ric's shoulder. "Go ahead."

"Are you sure?"

"Yeah. Just don't take too long letting us know how she is," Robert said.

His magnanimous gesture touched Ric. "Thanks, buddy."

Then he turned and followed the nurse back to the patient rooms.

*****

Kate's brain felt fuzzy as she lay on the hospital bed and closed her eyes. She heard the faint sounds of someone walking into her exam room and they touched her hand. Expecting it to be Robert, she was surprised when she opened her eyes and saw Ric. His eyes were filled with worry and his jaw tightened as he looked at her.

"Hi," she whispered.

"Hi. How are you feeling?" he asked, gently holding her hand.

She gave him a wan smile. "Like I hit a brick wall."

"Not funny, Doc. Not funny at all."

"Sorry. The doctor said that there's nothing broken and I don't have a concussion, but my back is scraped up pretty bad and I'm banged up good."

"That's right." An Asian man in scrubs came into the room. "Hi. I'm Dr. Zou."

"Ric Stanford, Kate's boyfriend. So, there are no fractures, nothing wrong with her spine?"

Dr. Zou shook his head. "Amazingly, no. I honestly expected at least a rib fracture, but Dr. Donoghue is one tough woman. She can go home, but no work for a week. I'll give you a prescription for a low dose of hydrocodone. I'll send it in with the nurse, along with your discharge papers."

"Thanks, Dr. Zou," Kate said.

He smiled and left the room.

"Please help me sit up so I can get dressed," Kate said.

Careful of her back, Ric assisted her into a sitting position while she swore and groaned. Her back burned and felt like she'd been pummeled.

Ric untied her gown and it fell away from her. "Jesus, Kate!"

"Looks that bad, huh?" she asked. "Doesn't feel too good, either."

Although he didn't say more, Kate saw the anger in his eyes. "Why are you so angry?"

"We are not talking about this here or while you're in this condition. Where are your clothes?"

His terse manner was just as bad as if he'd bitched her out, but Kate stayed calm. "They had to cut them off. They had me in a neck and back brace just in case."

His face paled even more at her words, but he didn't say anything. Having grown up around a lot of males, Kate knew that sometimes it was best to remain silent when they were upset. This was one of those times.

"They've given me scrubs to wear home."

Despite the fact that he was like a powder keg, ready to

explode at any second, Ric was extremely gentle as he helped her dress. By the time they'd finished, the nurse arrived with her discharge papers and script for the pain meds.

When she went to hand the clipboard to Kate to sign, Ric took it from her.

"Oh, sir, the patient needs to sign it," she said.

"I own this place," he said. "I guess my signature should suffice."

The nurse blinked at him.

"Ric Stanford. Nice to meet you, Sheila. I sign your paycheck," he said, smiling faintly as he signed the form. "There you go." He handed the clipboard back to the nurse and took the prescription from her. "Thanks."

Kate thought that poor Sheila looked like she was going to pee herself as she took the clipboard and left the room. "I can't believe that you just did that. I can sign a paper, Ric. Don't go all caveman on me, okay?"

He sighed. "Sorry. I'll go get a wheelchair."

Kate's temper flared. "I can walk, damn it."

Ric gave her his arm and made a broad sweeping motion towards the door with his other one. "Right this way."

She skewered him with a hard look and then stood up. Pain shot up her spine and she sucked in a breath and squeaked, "Okay. I'll take that wheelchair after all."

Ric chuckled as he helped her sit back down. "I thought you might."

"Bastard."

He grinned as he left the room and she called him more names in her head.

*****

Ric stayed with Kate until Tuesday, but once again, he

was called back to New York. Although he attended to business with his usual attention to detail, his mind was on Kate much of the time. He called her whenever he could to check on her and to make sure that she was behaving. Her body was healing, but she was still very sore.

The day after the accident, he'd put her in the bathtub twice, letting the hot water and bath salts soothe her as much as possible. He'd made her take her meds and had rubbed muscle ointment on her. Essentially, he'd treated her like a princess because he loved her so much and hated seeing her in pain.

During that week, he'd come to the realization that this would most likely not be the last time something like this happened. It was clear she was determined to stay a member of the rescue team. Kate prided herself on being fearless and not giving in to pain, and that included getting back in the saddle—or harness as the case may be.

For the first time since they met, Ric truly realized just how much risk Kate put herself in all the time. As a vet a well directed kick from a bull or horse and she'd be hurt. Let alone going into blizzards to rescue lost skiers, or helping stuck climbers down rock faces. He was terrified that she'd wind up dead, and he'd be left with another broken heart, torn apart by the death of another woman he loved.

He knew it wasn't fair but he compared Kate's lifestyle to Emily's. Why couldn't Kate be happy being a small animal vet and making a home with him? Why did she need thrills, why did she need more than him? He wanted to ask her not to climb, not to risk her life on silly pursuits, but what did that make him? Perhaps they were too different to be together The idea of his wife climbing...

By the time the weekend came, his brain buzzed with all of the thoughts going through it. It had been another bear of week both professionally and personally. As soon as he could on Friday, he left New York, anxious to get home to Kate.

Chapter Sixteen

Kate knew as soon as Ric arrived that night, that he had heavy thoughts on his mind. She'd been making a snack of apple slices and peanut butter when the dogs started barking and she heard his car pull in the driveway.

She smiled as she heard him greet the pooches.

"Kate? Where are you?"

"Kitchen!"

When he walked into the room, his shoulders were tense and his smile didn't quite reach his eyes.

"Hi, honey," she said. "You look like you had a bad day."

He gently embraced her and held her close for several moments. "I've had better. How are you feeling?"

Kate laid her cheek on his chest and breathed in his woodsy aftershave. He always smelled incredible and his muscular bulk was so nice to hold onto. "I'm fine. Almost all of the bruising is gone and I'm not very sore now. I'll be ready to go back to work tomorrow. I have so much to catch up on."

"I thought Dr. Zou said not until Monday?" Ric asked.

Kate drew away from him and went back to cutting apples. "He did, but I know my own body. I'm ready. You didn't wear your walking boot as long as you were supposed to, but I didn't bitch at you, did I?"

"I'm not bitching, Kate. I'm just concerned." He snatched an apple slice and popped it in his mouth.

"Are you hungry?"

"Starving."

Kate finished making her snack. "There's some leftover chicken salad in the fridge. You could make a sandwich."

"Okay. Sounds great."

He gathered the bread and chicken salad and then stopped, bracing his hands on the counter. "Kate, we need to talk."

Kate sat the apple slice she'd been about to eat back on the plate. "What about?"

"I'm not happy with the level of danger being involved with the mountain rescue team puts you in," Ric replied. "In fact, mountain climbing full stop sounds too dangerous. You were incredibly lucky this time, but you might not be so fortunate next time."

Kate folded her arms over her chest. "Ric, I'm an experienced climber, that's why I'm a valued member of the team. What happened wasn't my fault. There was no way to know that the lead line was defective."

Ric put his hands on his hips. "I know, but you almost died."

"Almost being the operative word. Ric, I know that this

was scary for you, but it was scary for me, too," Kate told him. "Besides, look what happened to Phil. He was killed by a drunk driver. You can't wrap yourself in cotton wool. Sometimes shitty things happen in life but that doesn't mean you don't live it."

Ric pursed his lips for a moment. "So you'll go back to climbing, you'll stay part of the rescue team, won't you?"

Kate nodded. "If everyone ran scared there would be no rescue team and it's sorely needed. I need to get back and climb as soon as I can. It's the old adage about getting back on a horse when you get thrown."

"I don't want you to."

She remained quite for a moment, before saying, "I love climbing. I'm not going to change my life because you think I should. No man is going to tell me what I can and can't do. Even one I love as much as you."

The sadness in Ric's eyes made Kate's heart hurt. "I love you, too, Kate. More than I thought I'd ever love anyone. But I can't be worried that when I'm not here, you're doing reckless, dangerous things. One of these days, something terrible is going to happen and I just can't stand by and watch it happen."

Kate's heart constricted. "What are you saying?"

"I'm saying that unless you're willing to quit rock climbing and the mountain rescue team, I can't keep seeing you." His grim expression held regret and pain.

"But you ride bulls and broncs," Kate said, trying to remain reasonable. "That's just as dangerous as climbing mountains."

Ric said, "I stopped when I was in college and got a dislocated shoulder. I still had Emily to help through college and I couldn't do that if I was dead or incapacitated. I just rope now, which isn't nearly as dangerous."

Indignation and anger flooded Kate. "Good for you." She shook her head. "I can't believe that you're giving me an ultimatum. I would never think to stop you doing what you love." I also thought Emily would have mentioned I was in mountain rescue.

"No, I didn't know about mountain rescue but I knew you climbed. I guess I didn't understand that what you did was so extreme," Ric said. "I can't lose someone again."

Kate went to him, putting a hand on his chest. "I'm not Lizzie, Ric. I'm not addicted to taking silly risks and I don't touch drugs well, not ones that aren't prescribed for me."

He took her hand and kissed her palm. "You share similarities. Lizzie thrived on danger and I'm wondering if part of the attraction for mountain climbing is the same with you—the thrill of beating the odds. I'm so sorry, Kate, but I'm just not prepared to sit by while you put yourself in danger. I hate to say it, but you have a choice: me or the mountains."

Agony clawed at Kate, but she wouldn't let him see it. "What if I demanded that you give up roping? Would you?"

Ric nodded. "If I knew that it really bothered you, yes. Can't you see my point of view? You have a decision to make, Kate."

She pounded the counter. "From what Emily and you have told me about Lizzie, I'm nothing like her. How dare you compare me with her? I have never compared you to Phil. That would not be fair."

"I'm simply being honest."

"Honest? Or running because things got real?"

Silence.

"Well, you do not get to order me around like I'm some teenager! I feel a calling to help with the rescue group. You're asking me to change, to cut out a part of me. I didn't stop driving a car when Phil died. This is no different."

"To me it is." He nodded calmly, which only pissed her off more. "I know how hard change can be. I was a good bull rider and I loved it. The excitement of not knowing what was going to happen when I sat on that bull, trying to outsmart it, to anticipate its every move.

"And how thrilling it was when I made it to the bell and heard the roar of the crowd. I know all about needing to feel the rush, but I had responsibilities that were more important than an eight-second joy ride. I'm not asking anything of you that I haven't done myself, Kate."

Kate wanted to scream and rail, but she held it together. He was making a good case. If she had a child would she risk life and limb, risk leaving her child motherless, just to climb? Was what Ric was saying right? "And just how long do I have to make this decision?"

Ric said, "I'll be back next weekend and you can let me know your answer then."

He put the sandwich makings back while she watched him in silence. Then he came to stand before her and the sorrow in his eyes was almost her undoing. She closed her eyes when he pressed a soft kiss to her forehead.

"Be well, Kate."

Kate's eyes remained closed as he left the kitchen. She couldn't bear to see him walk out. She heard him say goodbye to the dogs before the front door opened and shut. Only then did she give in to her grief. Her legs trembled and she sat down at the kitchen table because she was about to collapse. If Ric could walk away so easily, had he ever really loved her?

A numbing disbelief took hold of Kate as she sat there, going over what had just occurred. If you loved someone didn't you try and support what was important to them? Phil had never asked her to stop. She hated that she compared the two men because they were so different but Phil had loved her. She knew that. Did Ric?

How dare Ric ask her to give up something she loved so much? She felt part of the town and liked helping people. She wanted to think that if she were ever in trouble their were people who would rescue her. But she loved Ric, too. So much that she'd been increasingly fantasizing about a future together with him. But he was asking herself to give up a part of who she was in order to be with him. Could she? Would she?

Angry at the unfairness of her situation, Kate pushed to her feet, grabbed her snack, and headed for the living room. Sitting down, she turned on the TV and put on Hulu. She needed to get caught up on the last season of *Game of Thrones*, and watching it would be the perfect way to keep her mind off Ric and his ultimatum.

But ten minutes into the first episode, it became impossible to hold back her heartache, and a sob slipped out. She couldn't stop the thought that Ric did not love her the way she deserved to be loved and it cut her in two. Cinders scrambled onto the couch and wiggled his way into her lap. Kate hugged his solid little body and let her anguish pour forth.

*****

By Wednesday, Ric desperately needed to get drunk, but he didn't want to go with anyone from work and he hadn't made any close friends while he'd been in New York. He didn't want to get drunk on his own like some loser. He kept going over his words to Kate and the anger on her beautiful face. Was he wrong in wanting her to be safe?

Therefore, he decided to buy a couple of bottles of good scotch and get drunk at home, since all he had at home was beer. He ordered pizza and found a horror movie on Netflix. No way was he watching anything romantic. There was still no word from Kate and he had the sinking feeling that he wasn't going to hear from her again.

I shouldn't have gotten involved with her. I let my dick lead me around instead of keeping control of myself. But his feelings went so much deeper than just sex. There was only one thing about Kate that he didn't like: her need for danger. Too bad that it was a deal breaker for him.

He answered the door when the pizza guy got there and tipped him generously. Settling down again on the couch, he tried to pay attention to the movie, but his mind was too filled with Kate to pay close attention to the plot. For some strange reason, the blood and gore made him even sadder and he turned off the TV.

Needing a distraction, he opened his laptop and brought up Skype. He tapped Emily's icon and called her.

"Hey, big bro," she said with a smile. "What's up?"

"Make me laugh. I need to laugh." *Shit.* That wasn't what he'd intended to say, but it seemed as though the booze was already making him sentimental.

Her forehead puckered with concern. "Are you okay?"

"Yeah. Sure. I'm just bored and tired and my mind

won't shut down. Were you busy working?" he asked.

"You don't look very good," Emily said.

"Bad lighting and I'm working on getting drunk. I need to relieve some stress."

Sympathy shone in Emily's hazel eyes. "Tyler's been the same way with trying to juggle everything with the hospital and fighting this takeover attempt."

Ric snorted. "I'm about ready to say fuck it and just let them have it."

Shock crossed Emily's features right before the picture shifted to show Tyler. Ric recognized Emily and Tyler's bedroom now.

"What did you say?" Tyler asked, an odd look in his silver eyes.

"Shit. I didn't know you were there." He sighed and rubbed his eyes. "I'm tired, Ty, and the fact is that I miss home. God, listen to me whine. Don't mind me. I'm half-drunk. You know how I get."

Emily said, "Ric, don't blow smoke up our asses. This doesn't sound like you, drunk or not. What's wrong?"

His eyes filled with tears. "Kate and I broke up. At least, I'm pretty sure we're through."

Tyler must have pushed the laptop back farther on the bed because Ric could see both of them now. They looked at each other in surprise.

"Since when?" Emily asked.

Ric took a swig of scotch. "Friday."

"Start at the beginning," Tyler said, matter-of-factly.

Taking a steadying breath, Ric said, "Ty, you know that I was in love with Lizzie."

Tyler nodded. "You told me. But that was a while ago

now."

Ric let out a mirthless laugh. "I loved her because she was so full of life and brightened up any room she was in. Hayley reminds me so much of her."

Emily smiled. "Yes, she does."

"I tried not to love Lizzie after she led me on, played with my feelings when she needed me, but I never got over her. When she died, I almost hated her too. She thought life was one big joke. She took so many risks and didn't care who she hurt along the way. A piece of my heart went with her," Ric said. "I swore that I was never going to fall in love again and threw myself into my work."

Tyler said, "I know exactly what you mean. But then Kate came along, right?"

"Yeah. Out of the blue here comes this goddess in jeans, walking into your house that day and that was that. I just had to see her again," Ric said. "I know that things happened fast, but what I feel for Kate is so strong and real."

"If you love Kate so much, why would you break up with her?" Emily asked.

Gritting his teeth to keep from breaking into sobs, Ric got a hold on his emotions and told them everything. By the time he got to the end of the story, he felt a little lighter, but was just as miserable. "So the ball is in her court," he concluded. "And most likely, she's going to tell me to go to hell, or not talk to me at all."

Emily crossed her arms, resting them on her large belly. "I wouldn't blame her, Ric. I don't like the idea of her mountain climbing, either, but it's not my place to tell her she can't. Besides, what would happen if everyone decided that keeping safe was better than helping others. Where would our rescue team or our world be? It's not yours, either. Kate loves it because her dad taught her and her cousins when they were kids. Then her Dad died. That's why she grew up with her cousins. She feels close to her father when she climbs and closer to God, so she told me. You can't just ask her to give up something that means so much to her without talking it out."

Ric ran his hands nervously along his thighs. "We did talk about it. I asked her to give it up, she said she won't, and I can't be with someone who takes such risks with her life. When Robert called me that day, I thought he was going to tell me that Kate was dead. I can't go through that again. I just can't."

Tyler blew out a breath and rubbed the back of his neck. "Ric, Ric, Ric. When you love someone you have to love all of them. You don't let fear overrule that. We don't know what's going to happen down the road. Bad things happen to people when they're doing the most ordinary things. You broke your ankle just getting out of your car. That's not a dangerous activity, but you got hurt."

"Hell, Phil was killed driving to the store to pick up ice-cream," Emily added.

"I understand that," Ric said. "But constantly putting yourself in life-threatening situations is far different than having an accident. Kate was forty feet in the air. Forty feet! And she hand glides and cliff dives! She craves danger and I just can't be with someone who I'm going to constantly be worrying about. Not again. Could you guys?"

Emily shook her head. "How do you think I felt every time you guys got on a bull or bronco? I was so afraid that you'd snap your neck or be gored by an angry bull. And you dislocated your shoulder that one time!"

"Which is why I stopped riding them," Ric said. "I loved riding bulls and I wasn't a bit afraid while I was doing it, either. So, I get where Kate's coming from. I do. But I had to finish raising you and I wasn't going to get myself killed and leave you alone because I was too much of a thrill-seeker."

Tyler said, "I understand what you're saying, Ric, but I think you went about it all wrong. Most people don't respond well when they're given an order, especially when it involves personal matters." He and Emily exchanged a meaningful look. "For what it's worth, I think Kate's the one for you, Ric. You know it, too. You're the best negotiator I know. That's why we call you the Fixer. Are you willing to fight for your relationship with Kate, to work things out, or are you going to let fear and pride get in the way of your happiness?"

Ric took another pull from his bottle and nodded. "I know that I have some stuff to figure out."

"From the sounds of it, it involves more than Kate," Emily said.

Chuckling, Ric shook his head. "Before I broke my ankle and had to stay with you guys, I was perfectly happy here in New York. You remember how bored I was back in Cooper's Creek. All I could think about was business, all of the stuff I was going to have to catch up on. Now all I can think about is being back there with all of my family and friends."

"And Kate," Tyler said.

"Yeah," Ric said. "But even if it doesn't work out with her, I'd still rather be at least in Denver. I'm sorry, Ty, but my heart isn't in New York now. I only came here because I was running. Stupid of me."

"Running doesn't work." Emily nudged Tyler. "Does it, honey?"

Tyler wrapped his arms around her and kissed her cheek. "Nope. I learned that lesson, too."

Ric smiled glad to see them so happy.

"Do you want to sell to Lisbon?" Tyler asked.

Sitting the bottle of scotch on the coffee table, Ric said, "Not all of our company, just New York. Look, the fact is that we've got our hands full with the hospital and our investment clients in Denver and the West Coast.

"We've got plenty of money and we can probably work out something with Lisbon to keep our hand in the game a little here. I think we should diversify somewhat, though. Get into some other markets. We can do that from Denver and L.A. and come to the city when we need to. What do you think?"

Tyler grinned. "I think you're reading my mind. Lisbon is chomping at the bit so hard that I'm sure we can work out a great deal. Let's discuss it more tomorrow when we can get Chase in on the conversation, okay?"

"Sounds good," Ric said. "Thanks for lending me an ear. Goodnight, guys."

"'Night. Love you, bro," Emily said.

Ric smiled. "Love you, too, sis."

He hung up and closed his laptop. After taking a couple more swigs from his bottle, he lay down on the couch and picked up his phone. Bringing up his pics, he started flipping through all of the ones he'd taken of Kate.

His favorites were the couple that he'd taken while she'd

been asleep and those in which she was making silly faces. Smiling at the one where she was making an exaggerated model face, he wished to hell that he hadn't been so overbearing about the situation with her. Damn, but he missed her.

 The temptation to call her was almost too much to resist, but it was getting late and he was drunk. Not the right time to talk to her. With a sigh of regret, Ric sat the phone on the coffee table and closed his eyes.

 "Come on, Ric the Fixer. How are you going to fix this?"

 He needed to figure it out quickly or he was going to lose the best thing that had ever happened to him.

Chapter Seventeen

"Kate, you don't have to do this," Robert said.

They stood at the bottom of Elliot's Peak on Saturday, one of their favorite climbing locations. The view was killer and the climb was always challenging.

Kate checked her equipment one last time. "Yes, I do. I can't let it beat me."

Robert put a hand on her shoulder. "You have to be sure, Kate. You can't go up there with any reservations. You know that a half-hearted climber is a dangerous climber."

Kate met his eyes without flinching. "I'm ready. Let's go."

Her phone rang and her shoulders slumped. "Now, what?" Grabbing it out of her pack, a stab of surprise and longing ran through her when she saw Ric's smiling face on her lock screen. "It's Ric."

"I can see that," Robert commented wryly. "Are you going to answer it?"

"We're supposed to talk this weekend, but I don't see that there's anything to discuss. He doesn't want me to climb, but I love it and I don't want to give it up," Kate said. "He said that he can't—"

"I know all that. Don't rehash it. Don't answer that, okay?"

Kate let the call go to voicemail. "What is it?"

Robert leaned on the rock wall. "I don't like Ric giving you an ultimatum. You know that. But I know that he makes you happy. I love you too much to see you throw away that kind of love without at least talking to Ric more about it. I'm not saying that he's right. I'm just saying that you should hear him out. That said, he needs to listen to you, too. He was reacting out of fear from seeing you hurt, with a little more time maybe he'll think a little more rationally."

"Maybe. I don't know," Kate said. "Phil never had a problem with me climbing or doing anything, for that matter. We did everything together. Parasailing, hang gliding, climbing. I didn't know that this was going to be such a big hang up for Ric." She hesitated before saying, "Maybe Ric doesn't love me enough."

Robert fiddled with his water bottle. "Ric isn't Phil. Ric has never seen you climb or seen you do any of that other stuff to know how good you are at it. Now that his ankle is healed, you can start doing stuff like that together. Did you ever think about including him?"

It was a shock to Kate to realize that she hadn't. Why not? Ric was a big, strong guy who liked sports and physical activity. There were bound to be some things that he'd enjoying doing with her. If not rock climbing, there was always hiking. Hadn't he offered to teach her roping? Was it because she used to do those things with Phil and it had been their happy times? Was she subconsciously holding onto her past?

She shook her head. "That's not the point. He thinks I'm an idiot for doing a lot of the stuff I like to do."

Robert laughed. "A lot of people think we're crazy, but we don't get angry with them about it."

"They aren't trying to make us choose between our hobbies and them, though. That's what Ric's doing. Either I quit being an adrenaline junky, as he called me, or he can't be with me," Kate said. "I don't let anyone dictate what I can and can't do."

"I'm not saying you should," Robert said. "I'm saying that you have to be able to reach some sort of common ground."

"Why is this so important to you?"

"Because *you're* important to *me*. I want you to be happy. A second chance at true love doesn't come along every day, Special K. Is climbing some mountain really more important than building a life with the man you love?" Robert asked.

"It's the principle, Robert."

"So make him see that you're not going to be bossed around, but don't be so rigid that you can't compromise. I think that Ric's calling right now is a sign."

Kate laughed. "You're an idiot."

"No, I'm not. I'm a big believer in that sort of thing. You need to go talk to Ric instead of climbing today," Robert insisted.

Robert's earnest expression convinced Kate that he was completely serious. Maybe he was right. She'd been completely miserable without Ric. It had weighed on her heart and kept her awake. Forcing herself to be reasonable, Kate admitted that at least hearing what Ric had to say was the right thing to do.

She groaned and let her shoulders sag. "All right. Fine. I'll call him back."

Robert smiled. "Good decision. I'll start packing up our stuff."

Kate's stomach tightened with anxiety as she walked a short distance away. She hit Ric's icon and waited.

"Hi, Kate."

Just the sound of his voice made her feel weak. Kate told herself to remain strong. "Hi. I saw that you called. I didn't check my voicemail. I just called you back. What's up?"

"Well, I was wondering if we could get together this afternoon so we can discuss things?"

"I guess. What time?"

"Would it be okay if I picked you up around one?" he asked.

"Sure."

"Wear something old, Doc. See you then."

The line went dead and Kate looked at her phone in confusion. "What are you up to, Ric?"

*****

Kate waited outside for Ric. The sound of a loud motor reached her and she looked down the road. A big-ass camouflaged Hummer rolled up her driveway and Kate recognized the Beast. It came to a stop and Ric hopped down from it.

Her heart pounded at the sight of him in jeans and a Richard Petty T-shirt. He had to be the most delicious man on the planet. The determined set to his jaw and the heated gleam in his eyes made it impossible to look away from him as he walked up to her.

"You're looking good, Doc."

Biting the inside of her cheek to keep from giggling like a teenager, Kate looked him up and down. "You look okay, I guess."

He grinned at her frosty comment. "Ready to go?"

"Where are we going?"

"You'll see."

It was reminiscent of their first date. He'd kept their destination a secret from her then, too.

He held out a hand to her. "Come on. I'll help you in."

"I can get in on my own."

"Humor me. A gentleman always opens and shuts the door for a lady."

Kate rolled her eyes. "Fine."

He assisted her into the Beast and her whole body tingled from his touch. She'd missed him terribly. To distract herself from the sensations flowing through her, she looked around the interior of the vehicle.

She'd seen the Beast a couple of times, but she'd never been in it. All of the surfaces gleamed and the gray leather seats were spotless. Emily had told her that Ric was obsessed with keeping the Hummer spotless and in excellent running condition.

Ric nimbly climbed in and grinned at her. "Ready to go have some fun?"

"I thought that we were going to talk?"

"We can do both, can't we?"

Kate shrugged. "I guess."

He cranked the engine to life and Kate couldn't help smiling at the low, throaty growl of the engine.

Ric's grin flashed again. "Nice, huh?"

"Very nice," Kate admitted.

He put the H3 in drive and turned it around. "First off, I want to apologize for the way I acted last week. I was an ass and I owe you an explanation."

Kate said, "I'm listening."

He sobered as he pulled out onto the main road and headed away from town. "I need you to understand where I'm coming from with the whole climbing thing. You're a strong, capable woman, Kate. I love that you're fearless and that you don't back down from a challenge.

"I'd feel the same way if this was Tyler or Chase going climbing. I actually talked Chase out of skydiving last year because of the same sort of fear I have. You can ask him if you don't believe me."

Kate's expression turned dubious. "You talked Chase out of skydiving?"

"Yeah. You and him will get along really well because you're so much alike," Ric said. "He's always doing something that terrifies me. There are dangerous sports I'm okay with and then there are other sports that scare the hell out of me, like skydiving."

"Or climbing."

"Right," Ric said. "Kate, I'm just tired of losing the people I love. I lost my mom when I was thirteen. She had cancer and watching her slowly die was heart wrenching. My father started drinking because he couldn't accept Mom's death and he drank himself to death when I was twenty.

"My Uncle Johnny died overseas in Afghanistan, which

is how I wound up with the Beast. Then I lost Lizzie. Last year, I lost one very close buddy to cancer and another when he went deep sea diving. And just last month, we lost Smiley in that car crash. I'm just tired of death and funerals, Doc. Call me paranoid, but I get crazy when the people I love purposely put their lives on the line."

Her father was the only family member she'd lost but also at a young age, so she understood the pain. Phil's was the second person close to Kate who had ever died. She was fortunate to still have all of her grandparents and the rest of her immediate family. Ric had lived through seven significant deaths in the space of fourteen years. "I'm so sorry, Ric, but that still doesn't give you the right to dictate what I do with my life."

He fell silent as he turned down a road that was really no more than dirt tracks.

"Where are we?"

"We're going to Muddy's. She owns Muddy's Junkyard, but she also has a place where she lets people go boring around. She made an awesome off-road track and you can go on other trails, too."

Kate couldn't hold back her enthusiasm. "We're going mudding?"

"Yep, and you're going to drive," Ric said.

"You're going to let me drive? I haven't driven stick in a long time. I don't want to strip the transmission."

The lewd grin he sent her made her blood heat. "From what I've seen, you're great at driving stick."

She smacked his shoulder. "Shut the hell up."

He laughed as they came out of the woods to a huge field. A track with various obstacles and mud pits along its route sprawled across it. There was even a mountain of gravel to climb.

Kate's jaw dropped. "God, this is fantastic! It's an off-roader's dream!"

"We race here a lot," Ric said.

She hit his shoulder again. "You've been holding out on me!"

His laughter filled the cabin as he ducked away from her. "I wasn't going to let you come out here without me!"

Kate crossed her arms and stared out the passenger side window.

His light touch on her shoulder made her look at him again. "Kate, there are so many things that I want to share with you, but I can't do that if you're dead." The fear in his eyes made her heart squeeze. "I know that I can't tell you what to do, but as the man who loves you, who wants you in his life forever, I can ask you not to do outdoor climbing anymore.

"I know that you love climbing, and I wouldn't ask you to give it up completely. There are plenty of great indoor climbing places and I'll build you a climbing place if you want. It's the only thing you do that scares me so much. Okay, that's a lie. Cliff diving is the other thing that freaks me out. Hang gliding doesn't bother me, though. It sounds like fun. You could teach me."

She narrowed her eyes at him. "You're trying to negotiate a deal with me? What if I don't agree to give up climbing or cliff diving?"

*****

Ric had repeatedly asked himself that question and he had come up with one answer. "I will absolutely hate it if you keep doing those things, but I love you too much to tell you not to." He held up an index finger to keep her silent. "You're right. I'm trying to come to an agreement that we can both live with. Are you willing to discuss it?"

Her jaw tightened, but the curiosity in her eyes gave him hope that she'd capitulate that much. "Yes. I'm willing to talk about it."

"Good. If you stop climbing and cliff diving, I'm willing to give up bull and bronc riding for good. I was going to compete this past year, but I got hurt and couldn't," Ric said. "If there's something else I do that bothers you, I'll quit that, too. I want to be completely fair about this."

She made a wry face. "As far as I know, there's only one other thing you do that bothers me."

"What is it?"

"You have to be away so much. I understand why, but you being in a plane so much terrifies me about as much as me rock climbing does you."

Ric laughed. "You go hang gliding, but you don't like flying?"

"I know it's stupid, but that's how I feel. But there's no getting around that," Kate said.

"Well, actually, there is," Ric said. "Since you and I have gotten together, my heart is always here with you. New York isn't my home. It never was. I lived there, but I wasn't truly happy there. It was hard being so far away last year when Hayley was so sick and you see how hard it is for me to come home when I want to."

Kate nodded. "Or sometimes you have to leave on short notice."

"Right. I don't want to be in New York anymore.

Therefore, we're working on a deal to sell our New York division to Lisbon. I'm going to run the Denver office and Tyler's going to oversee things with the hospital. Chase loves L.A., and he's having a blast with all of the marketing, so he's staying put." Ric took her hand. "That way, I can be home most of the time and we can be weekend warriors together. What do you think?"

Ric calmly met her eyes, but anxiety gnawed at his stomach while he waited for her answer.

She chewed thoughtfully on her bottom lip and Ric almost groaned with the desire to kiss her. Would she accept or tell him to go to hell? His nerves stretched taut as he awaited her answer.

*****

Kate knew how hard it was to admit that you were wrong about something and she knew that Ric's apology was sincere. Now that he'd explained his position and why he was so uncomfortable with her climbing and cliff diving, Kate was sympathetic to his feelings. His compromise wasn't unreasonable. After all, he was giving up something, too.

It showed that he was a man of integrity and that he had a strong sense of fairness. She liked that he wasn't being demanding like he had been last week. His ultimatum had cut deeply and she'd been certain that they were through. Yet here he was asking her to reconsider and work things out.

Her resistance crumbled and tears filled her eyes as she nodded. "If you truly love me then I accept."

"I love you more than my next breath, that's why I reacted the way I did. I couldn't bear it if I lost you."

"I love you too."

"Are you sure?" Ric asked warily.

"Yeah. I'm very sure."

His arms came around her, pulling her hard against his chest, and his eyes locked on hers. "I'm so sorry, honey, and I'll never do that again," he promised. "I love you so much and I need you."

Winding her arms around his neck, Kate smiled as tears leaked from her eyes. "I accept your apology. I love you, too. And I need you."

The impulse to kiss him was too strong to resist. She pressed her lips to his sensual mouth and he immediately deepened the kiss. Kate reveled in the hungry way he devoured her lips and lightly stroked his tongue against hers. Need for him rose quickly and she leaned against him harder.

Ric abruptly broke the kiss. "God, Kate, I want you so much. I missed you. Not just our lovemaking, but just being with you."

"I've missed you, too. I want you. Make love to me," she said.

Ric looked around. "We're a little too out in the open here." He turned the ignition on again. "But I know the perfect place to go where we'll have some privacy."

As he put the Hummer in gear, Kate reached over and ran her hand up his thigh until she encountered a bulge under his jeans. She rubbed and played with it. Ric groaned and drove faster.

"Doc, I hope you're not going to need a lot of foreplay, because I don't think I can wait," he said as he turned down another dirt track that ran through thick forest. Suddenly, he whipped the wheel to the right and they plowed through low hanging tree branches until it seemed as though the forest had swallowed them up.

He stopped and put the Beast in park. As he reached for her, he smiled and a soft light shone in his eyes. "I'm never going to let you get away, Kate. You're the woman I've been waiting for all my life and I don't want to ever be without you. You're everything I could ever want in a woman and so much more. Katherine Rose Donoghue, the woman I love more than life itself, will you do me the huge honor of becoming my wife?"

Kate's heart felt like it was going to leap right out of her chest. Was she dreaming or had Ric just proposed to her? She could only stare at him as he produced a ring from his jeans pocket and held it in front of her. It was a breathtaking Princess cut diamond nestled inside of a cluster of tiny diamonds.

"Kate?"

Looking into Ric's eyes, Kate saw his powerful love for her and her heart echoed that love. She was ready. Ready to risk her heart again because of this man. It was Ric who brought life back to her and of course love. "Yes, Ric, I'll marry you."

His eyes misted over as he slipped the ring on her finger. It shimmered when she moved her hand.

"It's gorgeous," she said.

He took her hand and looked at the ring on her finger. "I'm so glad you like it. I promise to make you happy for the rest of our lives, Kate. You'll never have to wonder how much I love you."

Kate brushed away his tears even as some trickled down her own face. "You already make me happy. I want to share everything with you and I can't wait to start our life together."

Ric's mouth descended on hers with the power of a tornado and her senses spun with the force of her desire for him.

When the kiss ended, she said, "I want you now. I can't wait."

Ric grinned and got out.

"Where are you going?"

He opened the passenger seat door and started putting the back seats down. "I'm making room for us." Then he hopped in and pulled open one of the cargo compartments in the back. He brought out a sleeping bag and spread it out. A pillow was also in the compartment and Ric situated it before closing the compartment.

"Okay, Doc. Get that sweet ass back here."

Kate squirmed between the bucket seats until she could crawl back to him. He already had his underwear and jeans down around his knees. His cock jumped a little as he hardened before her eyes.

His eagerness for her was the only foreplay she needed. Hastily, she undid her jeans and shoved them over her hips. She got them as far as her knees before Ric pulled them up over his shoulders and settled his hips between her thighs.

"I love you, Kate."

Kate reached down to touch him, loving the way he felt in her hand. "I love you, too. You feel so good. I want you inside me."

Ric pulled a condom out of his pocket and opened it. Kate took it from him and rolled it down his rigid shaft. "You're so hard, baby," she said.

"I can't help it. That's what you do to me."

Kate lay back and lifted her hips to him. "Come on, cowboy."

She watched as Ric guided himself inside her. It was so erotic to see his body joined with her. Exquisite pleasure filled her as he buried his cock deep. Pulling his head down for a kiss, she said, "Make me come. I need you so much."

His growl reverberated along her nerves, heightening her excitement even more. Laying down on her, Ric gathered her to him and began moving his pelvis slowly.

"Harder," she whispered. "Faster."

Ric immediately complied, thrusting harder against her. It was exactly what she needed. She was wild for him and moved with him. Locking her legs around him, she clutched at him as they soared higher. Ric's hips moved like pistons and he slammed against her over and over.

"Touch yourself, Kate. It's so fucking hot when you do that. I love knowing that you have pleasure two ways at once." His voice was rough with passion and his breathing was harsh.

With a sultry smile, Kate slid her hand down until she could touch where they were joined. Then she found her clit and lightly stroked it.

"That's it, sweetness," Ric said. "I want to come with you. Tell me when you're there. I want to make you feel so good."

His control always amazed Kate. He never let himself climax until she had.

Between his pounding thrusts and her strokes, it didn't take long to reach the brink. "Ric, I'm going to come. Yes. Now! Now!"

Ric's movements became frenzied and drove her over the

edge into a release that made her feel as though she was being fantastically shattered. Kate screamed his name as he found his own pleasure.

"Oh, God, Kate," he rasped out. "It's incredible. You're incredible."

Kate couldn't speak for the intense sensations flooding her body. A high-pitched moan escaped her as she shook under him as ecstasy overtook her. Gradually, she drifted back to Earth and Ric slowly collapsed on her.

She loved feeling his weight and wrapped her arms around him as they caught their breath. "I really like this off-roading. I hope we come here a lot."

Ric laughed and raised his head to look at her. "We'll definitely come back. You drive me crazy."

Kate kissed him. "You drive *me* crazy."

Carefully, Ric disentangled himself from her with a chuckle. "We never even got our pants off."

Kate giggled. "I know. Damn, that was hot."

"Mmm. It sure was," Ric agreed.

They dressed and drove back to the track where Ric had Kate switch him places. He grinned and she loved the excitement in his eyes. "Ready for this?"

Kate took a firm hold of the wheel and smiled back at him. "As long as I have you, I'll be ready for anything."

He kissed her briefly. "You'll always have me. Okay, put it in gear and let her rip!"

As Kate took them around the course, she felt as though they were driving into a new adventure. *Aren't we*, she thought. Kate started up the gravel mountain, and she and Ric hollered and laughed as the Hummer's wheels caught hold, propelled them towards the top.

At the summit, they sat there a minute looking down at the world below them. Then she moved them forward and they started the descent. It was exhilarating and challenging, much like Kate felt the future would be. As they bounced down the gravel mountain, Kate couldn't wait to see what adventures awaited her and her rugged cowboy.

Epilogue

Ric and Kate's wedding, which was held outdoors at the Jeffries, took place on the third weekend in July. Kate had wanted a completely different ceremony than the one that she and Phil had planned.

She and Ric loved seeing each other in jeans, which had gotten Kate thinking. Ric might be wise to the way of the city and look hot in a suit, but he would always have the heart of a country boy. So, instead of a large church affair, she'd opted for a blue jean wedding because she thought it fit their relationship better.

Despite Robert's initial protests, Kate had talked him into being her man of honor. Even though she was seven months along now, Emily had jumped at the chance to be Kate's bridesmaid. She'd never worn a blue jean dress and was excited about it.

As Kate stood in front of the full-length mirror in Emily's room, she admired the light-weight blue denim, off-the-shoulder dress. It was an old-fashioned design with a tight-fitting bodice and full skirt. Lacy ruffles edged the bodice and the bottom of the skirt. Small rhinestones glittered along the bodice, adding sparkle to the dress.

Her grandfather, Angus, came into the room and smiled at her reflection. "You look like a cowgirl angel."

She grinned and turned to him, smiling up into eyes so like her own. She was the mirror image of Angus and Kate adored him. "Thank you. Look at you! So handsome."

Angus spread his arms wide. "Not bad for an old coot."

Her grandfather was a powerfully built man, and he cut quite a figure in his dark blue jeans, red Western shirt and black string tie.

"You look great. I'm so glad you approve of Ric," she said. "I was worried that you wouldn't."

"What's not to like? He loves my little girl like crazy and he's rich," Angus remarked.

Kate straightened Angus' tie a little. "I'm not marrying him for his money, Granddad."

"I know that, but it doesn't hurt." He held up his hand. "I know, I know. Your practice is doing just fine. Your mother and the family are so proud of you. Your Dad would have been especially proud."

"Thank you. I know he's here with me." And she'd been to Phil's grave that morning and spoken with him. Somehow she knew Phil was happy for her.

"Well, Sunshine, are you ready to go marry your cowboy?"

Kate's smile could've lit up the room. "I'm nervous, but I can't wait."

"Let's go then."

He led her out of Emily's room and down the stairs. Emily and Robert were waiting for them in the kitchen.

Robert grinned at her. "Look at you, Special K! You look so beautiful."

"Yes, you do," Emily said. "Who knew that denim could be so pretty?"

Her own dress resembled Kate's, but had a shorter skirt so she didn't trip on it.

Kate hugged Robert. "Thanks again for doing this. You're my best friend and I wanted you to stand up with me."

"Happy to do it," Robert said.

"You look very handsome, too."

He straightened his blue denim vest, which he wore with a white dress shirt, dark blue jeans and pair of black cowboy boots. "Why thank you, ma'am."

They laughed at his poor imitation of Chase's accent.

"Come on all of you," Angus said. "We don't want to keep everyone waiting."

As Kate stepped outside and took Angus' arm, she tried to quell the butterflies bumping around in her stomach. There was nothing to be nervous about. She was marrying the man who'd captured her heart with his mesmerizing blue eyes and captivating grin. The man who would be by her side forever and become the father of her children.

Looking at Emily, who lovingly placed a hand on her swollen belly, Kate hoped that she and Ric would conceive soon. Putting that out of her mind for the moment, though, she concentrated on the present and walked beside her grandfather with joy in her heart.

*****

As he waited for his bride, Ric worked on bringing his heart rate down so that he didn't sweat through his white shirt. He didn't know why he was so nervous. The wedding was going off without a hitch so far. They had enough chairs for all the guests, the food was taken care of, and the band was set up and ready. Perhaps, because half the town was here.

Tyler put a hand on Ric's shoulder. "It'll be okay, Ric. That's what you told me on my wedding day, remember?"

"Yeah," Ric nodded. "I can't figure out why I'm ready to jump out of my skin. I love Kate more than anything and I want to spend the rest of my life with her."

Tyler chuckled. "Tucker told me that choosing a wife is the most important decision a man will ever make. It's a very serious step in your life, but it's also the happiest. Trust me about that, Ric. Everyone can see how much you and Kate love each other. That's the most important thing and it'll get you through the tough times."

"Well, listen to Mr. I-used-to-have-ice-in-my-veins waxing poetic about love," Chase piped up with a grin.

Ric laughed as Tyler's expression darkened. "He's got you there, Ty."

Tyler smiled a little sheepishly. "Well, a certain hot blonde melted the ice in my veins in more than one way."

Ric put his hands over his ears. "I don't want to hear about that!"

Chase and Tyler laughed at his reaction just as Hayley started walking down the aisle. She sprinkled rose petals as she led Coco. A small pillow holding the wedding rings had been attached to Coco's collar.

Hayley beamed as she approached the altar, proud to have been chosen as the flower girl. She looked adorable in her frilly jean dress. When her and Coco reached the altar, Ric hugged her and praised her for doing such a good job. Tyler and Chase agreed and Tyler untied the rings from Coco's collar. Then Hayley and Coco went to sit with Brooke and Tucker.

Emily appeared at the end of the aisle created by the white wooden chairs. Ric watched Tyler's gaze focus intently on her and he was glad his sister and one of his best friends had found happiness together. The way Emily blushed under Tyler's close scrutiny was sweet.

As Emily arrived at the altar, Ric stepped over to her and gave her an impulsive hug. "You look gorgeous, sis."

"Thank you. You look fantastic," she said.

"I know," he said, winking.

Emily rolled her eyes and shooed him away. He rejoined his co-best men just as Robert started walking down the aisle. It was strange seeing a man over on the bride's side, but it made complete sense that Kate had chosen Robert as her man of honor.

Ric would always be grateful to him for saving the woman he loved from the jaws of death. Any jealousy he'd felt towards Robert had faded and he was glad that Kate had someone else who was always on her side. Robert smiled at him and took his place by Emily.

Tyler nudged Ric and pointed towards the end of the aisle. Ric's gaze followed the direction he'd indicated and his heart stopped as he got his first glimpse of Kate in her wedding dress. Her slim, toned figure was shown off to perfection by the blue jean dress she wore and Ric knew that no other woman would ever compare to her.

Desire and love mingled in his heart and his anxiety fled as Kate walked to him. Her dark eyes sparkled with love and appreciation and her sweet lips curved in a beautiful smile. She wore her hair scooped up on top of her head with curly tendrils framing her face.

Ric had been so engrossed in Kate that he hadn't paid much attention to Angus, but when they reached the altar, the older man gave Ric a warning look that clearly said that he'd kill Ric if he didn't take good care of Kate. Ric gave Angus a brief nod to reassure him and then took Kate's hands.

*****

Looking into Ric's eyes, Kate couldn't believe that she was marrying this gorgeous man. The way he filled out his jeans and shirt made her mouth go dry and made her think thoughts that she shouldn't while standing so close to a pastor. His loving, hot gaze made her feel a little weak and she had to take deep breaths to clear her mind.

The roguish smile that curved his lips told her that he was having much the same thoughts. Then the pastor started the ceremony and Kate concentrated on her vows. This was the only time she ever planned on getting married and she made each word count as she promised to love and honor Ric.

Hearing him say those words back to her was a magical experience and Kate could hardly contain all of the joy she felt inside. As they exchanged rings, her heart healed even more. Even though she would always love and miss Phil, she knew that she was no longer *in* love with him. She'd said her goodbyes at the cemetery this morning.

No, the man sliding a gold wedding band onto her finger was now the man she loved. He'd given her the courage to step out on the ledge where love was concerned and she knew that he'd always be there to catch her.

Pastor Dan Porter said, "You may now kiss your bride."

Ric cupped her face and her pulse leapt at the contact. When their lips touched, Kate's eyes shut on happy tears that leaked out from under her eyelids. It was a sweet and sensual kiss that held love and the promise of a lifetime of happiness.

Suddenly, Ric dipped her and Kate let out a squeal of surprise while the congregation whistled and clapped approvingly. She wound her arms around his neck and kissed Ric back, which only caused more laughter and catcalls.

When Ric let her up, Kate felt a little dizzy from the sensations he elicited in her.

He hugged her close. "I love you so much, Dr. Stanford."

"I love you, too, Mr. Stanford," she replied, grinning.

A swarm of well-wishers interrupted them and they turned their attention to their guests.

*****

Once the bride and groom were seated at their table, Tyler stood up and got the guests' attention. He held several index cards, which Ric saw Chase eyeing.

Chase looked up at Tyler. "How long is this speech? Some of us are hungry, you know," he said loudly.

Ric and Kate muffled laughs as Tyler glared at Chase, who kept glancing questioningly at the index cards. The guests laughed outright and Tyler couldn't keep a smile off his face. "If you're that hungry, you know where the food is."

Chase shrugged and got up. "Okay."

Tyler's jaw dropped as Chase walked over to the area where a BBQ had been set up. "I can't believe he really left before my speech. Get back here!"

Chase already had a plate with a barbequed chicken leg on it. He picked it up and gestured towards Tyler. "Go ahead. You got a big mouth, so I'll be able to hear you from here."

Loud laughter followed this announcement, Tyler's included. Ric had to admit that Tyler was taking Chase's insults with good humor. Of course, it was hard to be offended by Chase because he was so charming and funny.

About halfway through Tyler's speech, which was interspersed with insults from Chase, it became apparent to Ric that it was a little skit that the two of them had cooked up. It was hilarious and everyone had tears in their eyes from laughing so hard.

Kate's instincts about their ceremony and reception had been spot on and Ric knew that he wouldn't be enjoying himself nearly as much as if they'd had a traditional wedding. The food was delicious and it was amusing to see everyone wearing huge bibs so they didn't get barbeque sauce all over their clothes.

When the time came for the dancing, Chase hopped up on the temporary band stage and took one of the mics. Ric and Kate had asked him to sing the song for their bride and groom dance. He'd agreed, but only if he was allowed to pick their song. They'd agreed to his terms and had been curious about what Chase was going to sing. However, no amount of pleading had convinced Chase to reveal his choice.

"Can I have everyone's attention, please?" Chase asked.

One of the band members gave him a stool and his acoustic guitar while the crowd quieted. He situated himself on the stool and said, "My granddaddy was the smartest person I've ever met and he used to say that sometimes it takes a while to find true love, but that most people eventually get there if they're smart enough to pay attention." He strummed softly on the guitar as he spoke.

"Granddaddy told me that there might be some bumps along the way and maybe you'd get bogged down by troubles and sorrow a couple of times. But he said that the day would come when the sun would come out and light your way to the path you were meant to go down."

He smiled at Ric and Kate. "You two have run into some pretty big bumps in the road and hit a couple of patches of heartache, but it's my firm belief that on the day y'all met, the skies cleared, the sun came out, and pointed you down the path to everlasting love. Which is why I chose this as your bride and groom dance song."

His picking turned into the introduction of Rascal Flatt's, *Bless the Broken Road*. The hair stood up on Ric's neck as he realized just how perfect the song was for them. He saw that Kate was thinking the same thing.

In an old-fashioned gesture, Ric bowed to Kate and kissed her hand, before pulling her into his embrace. When Chase started to sing, Ric felt the words pierce him because they so accurately said what he felt for Kate.

His love for Lizzie had blinded him to the possibility of there being someone out there who would want and love him. Someone who would completely give him her heart and heal the wounds in his. Kate was a woman he could build a life with. They were a team. Working together, learning to compromise, and most importantly giving each other unconditional love. He never thought he'd find his soul mate but when he'd least expected it, the love of his life had found him and she'd taken away the pain of his past.

*****

Kate closed her eyes and rested her head on Ric's shoulder as she listened to Chase sing.

Although she hadn't been able to see it at the time and she still might not completely understand why, Phil hadn't been her true path. She'd loved him with all of her heart and she believed that they would've been happy.

But, for whatever reason, he hadn't been the one she was meant to spend her life with. She doubted she'd ever reconcile why he'd had to die, but Ric's understanding and compassion had helped heal a lot of her anger and had showed her that his love was worth risking another broken heart.

She lifted her gaze to Ric's and thought about how Robert had thought he'd heard Phil the day she'd fallen. Maybe he really had and Phil was the one who'd led her to Ric. Could he have wanted them to meet because he'd known they would be perfect for each other? Knowing Phil, she wouldn't put anything past him. She broke into a smile as Ric mouthed the last verse to her.

It amazed her how two people who'd lived through such tragedy had found their way to each other. What had started out as just a casual fling had fast become so much more. In each other, they'd found healing and love, joy and their best friend. They'd found the strength to pull out of the pride-filled rut they'd gotten stuck in and push through their hurt feelings so that they could reach a compromise.

As the song ended and Ric pressed a kiss to Kate's lips, sunshine flooded her soul, erasing any lingering cracks in her heart. That light stayed with her throughout the rest of the reception and, from the loving looks and smiles he sent her, Ric felt it, too.

It wasn't long after they'd tried to smear cake into each other's faces and had eaten their fill of cake that they decided to leave for their honeymoon. Just as they'd gone for a nontraditional wedding, they'd opted for a different kind of honeymoon. They'd rented a cabin in the Rockies for a couple of weeks and planned to go hiking and fishing.

The Beast had been tricked out in pink and camo streamers and a sign saying, "Just Hitched" had been hung on the back of it.

There was one thing Kate wanted to do before they left. She got everyone together and threw her bouquet. She heard the squeals and when she turned to see who had caught it, her heart lifted when she saw Brooke with one hand gripping the stems while Robert held the satin ribbon. Now that could be a good pairing.

"You did that on purpose," Ric teased.

"Sometimes love needs a helping hand."

"That it does," and Ric handed Kate up into the vehicle and made sure that her dress wouldn't get in the way of the door before shutting it. Then he hopped up in it and turned the ignition. He and Kate hung out of the windows, waving at everyone for a minute before they started down the driveway, heading towards a lifetime of adventures.

*****

Chase watched the newly married couple drive off and the happy face-mask he'd worn all night slipped.

"Don't worry, Chase, you'll be next. Two down and one to go," Tucker said as he thumped Chase on his back as he went past.

Everyone had been saying that to Chase all evening.

He wouldn't be next. There would be no happy family for him. Once women learned he couldn't have children they fled. It was safer to stick to his party girls. They simply wanted him for his money and body. He was okay with that because that's all he had to give.

He stood watching until the Hummer drove out of sight. He took a swig from his beer bottle and turned to go in and help Ty clear up.

Sneak Peek at Want Me, Coopers Creek #3

Chapter One

Pulling into a visitor's parking spot in front of the office building, Anna Spencer wondered if she'd gotten the wrong place until she saw the huge Horizon Enterprises sign on the side of the small skyscraper. Unlike other office buildings in the area, the windows were tinted different colors. The sun glinted off the glass surfaces, creating a rainbow effect.

Anna looked at the windows and then at the Horizon logo. It depicted a low mountain range with the sun rising over one of the peaks. Anna had to smile at the way the colorful rainbow accentuated it. Leave it to Chase McIntyre to create a marketing advert from an actual building. She got out of her Honda Accord, grabbed her briefcase from the backseat, and headed for the door.

Anna was surprised when she had to submit to a metal detector test, but cooperated. The guard pointed her to the elevators and she thanked him. Stepping onto one, she straightened her light gray power suit and hoped that she wasn't sweating like a pig. She was nervous enough about meeting Chase without the added stress of worrying about bad b.o.

She got off on the eleventh floor and checked in with Chase's secretary, a middle-aged woman with dishwater blonde hair.

"Hello. I'm Anna Spencer from Innovative Graphics. I have an eight o'clock appointment with Mr. McIntyre," she said, smiling.

"Oh, yes. He said to bring you upstairs. My name's Ginger."

"It's nice to meet you, Ginger," Anna said.

Ginger led her back to the elevator and punched the button that said "roof".

"Why are we going to the roof?" Anna asked, tucking a few strands of wavy auburn hair behind her left ear.

"Because that's where Chase is," Ginger said simply.

"Oh. Okay."

Anna didn't question the woman any further, but she wondered why the meeting would take place atop a skyscraper.

Ginger said, "Now, I should warn you about Chase. He's not like other executives. He's a little unusual."

"So I've heard." Anna smiled. "I've done my homework on him."

Ginger nodded. "Good. Then I don't need to tell you any more."

Presently, they arrived at the top and the elevator doors opened. Anna blinked and thought she'd entered an alternate universe. What looked like a tropical island lay outside the elevator.

Ginger laughed. "I'm sorry, but I just love seeing people's reactions when they see it for the first time. This is what Chase calls the Roof Top, his boardroom slash…well, you'll see."

They stepped out onto what looked like short grass and

walked along a meandering path through tall plants and a few small tropical trees. Anna looked back and saw that the elevator doors had been painted to resemble a bamboo gate.

Ginger led her out of the foliage to where a long wooden table sat, shaded by a large green-and-white canopy. Wicker chairs with thick green cushions were situated around it and a laptop and cellphone lay at the head of the table. The outdoor setting was as nice as anything she'd ever seen at a resort.

"Chase!" Ginger called out. "Your guest is here!"

Anna wasn't sure what to make of being called a guest, but she refrained from commenting.

"All right! Be right there!" a man shouted back.

"Shake a leg, Chase! People don't have all day!" Ginger groused.

"Yes, ma'am."

Ginger shook her head. "I swear being his secretary is more like being his mother. He'll be along. Good luck."

"Thank you," Anna said with a tight smile.

Ginger got back on the elevator, leaving Anna alone standing next to the table. She'd seen pictures of Chase and his work for Horizon, so she knew that he was gorgeous. Looking down at herself, she grimaced at her rather plain attire and wished she would've worn something a little sexier. *Knock it off. You're here for a business meeting, not a date.*

"Hi. Sorry to keep you waiting, Miss Spencer."

Anna jerked her gaze from her shoes up to meet the most gorgeous eyes she'd ever seen. They brought to mind dark chocolate and the rest of the man was just as delicious. A slightly aquiline nose led down to utterly beautiful male lips that were made for kissing. His strong, angular jaw was clean-shaven and he smelled like rain and tropical fruit.

He wasn't overly tall, maybe somewhere around six-foot, but he seemed larger than life to Anna. His broad, brawny shoulders and wide chest tapered down to trim hips. Although his cargo shorts hid his thighs, they must be powerful judging by his muscular calves. His light caramel skin tone perfectly complemented his eye color and long, dark brown hair.

He held a large pitcher of some sort of fruit juice and a tray of glasses. "Just let me sit these down."

Anna took the opportunity to compose herself when he turned and placed the tray and juice on the table. Facing her again, he smiled and Anna felt on the verge of swooning. *What's the matter with you? Get a grip!*

He held out a hand. "Chase McIntyre at your service, Miss Spencer."

His hands were the most beautiful male hands Anna had ever seen. They looked strong and masculine, yet they were nicely shaped. Anna could imagine what they'd feel like on her skin.

Anna put her hand in his and was surprised at the warm, almost intimate way he shook it. He closed his fingers around hers and met her gaze with those incredible eyes that held equal amounts of kindness, humor, and confidence.

"It's wonderful to meet you, Mr. McIntyre." Anna hoped that he didn't notice that her voice was a little breathy.

"Likewise." He released her hand and motioned towards the table. "Have a seat. Make yourself comfortable. The rest of the gang will be along in a bit, but I thought it would be good to talk privately at first."

Anna tried to get her pulse under control as she walked over to a chair next to the head of the table, where his things sat. She was surprised when he helped seat her. It had been a long time since a man had done that for her.

"Thank you."

"No sweat." Chase sat down and proceeded to pour two glasses of juice, sliding one over to her. "Mango, avocado, and pineapple. I just squeezed it fresh. Great for vitamin C and antioxidants."

"Thanks."

Chase took a healthy swig and sat his glass down. "So, how are you today?"

"I'm fine and yourself?"

"Well, I had a great surf earlier and Lola had a great swim, so I'd say that the day is off to a good start," Chase replied.

The image of Chase rising from the sea in only skin tight swim trunks made Anna choke a little on her juice. He wasn't the type of man she'd normally lust after. Rich and powerful men—well, she'd been there and done that and barely lived to tell the tale.

Chase reached over and patted her on the back. "You okay?"

"Yes. Sorry." What on earth was wrong with her today? Horizon, or Chase McIntyre was an important client. Her boss, and the other three members of the firm's staff were counting on her getting this job. Tom's last words to her were "do whatever it takes to impress McIntyre and get that contract".

When she'd asked what he'd meant by "whatever", Tom's expression had left no doubt in her mind that he'd actually meant *anything*. The firm needed the money this contract would bring and she needed her salary to stay one step ahead of her ex. The restraining order only afforded her so much protection and the police had informed her that they'd done everything that they could.

Chase grinned. "So, I'll bet that you have some stuff for me to look at."

Anna picked up her briefcase and pulled out the mock-ups she'd brought for business cards, brochures, and other promotional material. Horizon had decided to outsource those products and Anna was confident that Chase would be impressed by her designs.

She slid them over to him. "As you can see, I—"

Chase held up a silencing hand. "Not to be rude, but just let me get a first impression of them. Sort of like looking at art. No explanation, just let me feel the emotion."

His southern accent slid like silk across her nerves. "Okay."

While Chase perused the materials, Anna looked around to keep from staring at him. She wondered what was beyond the outdoor boardroom. It was hard to tell with all the tall foliage blocking her view.

"Um, I'm sorry, darlin', but none of these are gonna work," Chase said.

She tried not to let the word 'darlin'' annoy her. Anna's mouth dropped open as she turned her attention back to Chase. "Excuse me?"

"I don't think Tom understood what I told him on the phone last week," Chase said. "Did you do these?"

Heat suffused Anna's cheeks. "Yes. I spent a lot of time on them."

Chase nodded. "I thought so and they're fantastic, but not for Horizon. I know several firms that these would work for and I'll be happy to recommend you to them. I told Tom that we're rebranding and that we're after something different, something friendlier. We don't want to be one of those boring old, stuck-up investment companies anymore. We want people to feel like we're their friends, not their brokers and bankers."

Anna couldn't believe that all her painstaking research had been done in vain. She'd thought Chase would be like any other rich, handsome playboy. The glitzier, and the more glamorous the style, the better. Where had she gone wrong? Had she let her experience with her ex blind her?

Mortified, Anna started packing up her samples as she inwardly fumed. She was going to kill Tom for not giving her more details. "I'm so sorry for wasting your time, Mr. McIntyre. I had no idea that was the direction you were going in."

He gently took hold of her wrist to stop her. "What are you going to do with those?" He pointed to the mock-ups.

"I…well, I'll throw them away." Her heart skipped a few beats at his touch. She was about to pull her hand away but his light hold disappeared as he picked up her work.

"No, no. I'll put them in our mixed-paper recycling," Chase said. "I make our employees recycle everything. Bottles, plastic, cans, and paper all get recycled. Our planet is dying, but I'm gonna do my part to keep it going as long as possible."

He had to be one of the strangest playboys Anna had ever encountered and he put her on edge. She hated that he was so unpredictable.

"Fine. You can have them." Most rich men only thought about themselves. That made them easy to handle because she knew what to expect. Reading Chase was like being blind and trying to read a normal printed book.

Chase put them in a neat stack to the left of his laptop. "Thanks." He got up and held out a hand to her. "Now, take a walk with me."

*****

"A walk with you? Why?"

She was like a skittish foal—*interesting*. Chase gave her a disarming smile and watched Anna's shoulders relax a little. He felt bad for her and wanted to put her at ease. "So you can get a sense of who we are now so you can start over. You still want the job, don't you?"

Anna nodded curtly. "Absolutely."

"Awesome." He stood up and let out a whistle. "Lola! C'mon!"

A huge Bernese Mountain dog came trotting out of the shaded tropic garden and looked at Chase expectantly.

"Lola, say hello to Anna," he said.

Lola barked as she looked up at Anna.

"Hi, Lola. Gosh, she's big," Anna said, bending down to pet her head a shade tentatively.

"She's big but as gentle as a lamb," Chase said. "Aren't you girl?"

Lola responded to Chase with a soft woof.

"I love dogs." Anna laughed as she gave Lola a final pat. "I'm a country girl at heart and she's bigger than any lamb I've ever seen. I grew up on a farm in Iowa and then we moved to a little town outside of Denver. We always had pets."

Chase said, "Really? What town?"

"Cooper's Creek."

His eyes widened. "You're kidding."

Anna shook her head. "No. I graduated high school there."

"So did I."

Her smile was full of disbelief. "Yeah, right."

"No, I really did. I don't remember you. You must be a few years younger than me. I graduated in 2005. Ate at the Diner all the time and you gotta know Tucker," Chase said.

Anna's stunning green eyes lit up. "Tucker McGee? He fixed all of our cars." She shook her head a little. "I can't believe this. I have to confess that I did a little investigating about you, but there was no mention of where you grew up."

Chase's smile faded a little. "Well, I don't put it out there for the public. I lived in Texas until I was about fourteen and then I moved to Cooper's Creek."

Anna gasped and grabbed his arm. "You're *that* Chase McIntyre?"

Her soft palm on his arm and the excited look on her beautiful face kicked Chase's libido into gear. "Depends on which Chase McIntyre you mean. If it's the bad Chase, then, no, I'm not him," he joked.

She laughed and the pretty sound made his groin tighten a little. "The football player. Best wide receiver Cooper's Creek has ever had."

Chase grinned. "That's me, all right."

Anna looked at where she still held his arm, and suddenly sobered and let go. "I'm so sorry. I just got excited to meet someone from my hometown."

"That's okay. I don't mind being grabbed by pretty

women." The shocked look on her face made him quickly amend his statement. "I meant that I don't mind being touched by—shit, that's no better than the first thing I said. I meant nothing sexual by that."

His discomfort must have pacified Anna because her stern look dimmed and those pretty lips of hers curved into a smile. "And I don't go around grabbing handsome men."

Chase could believe that. She seemed slightly stuck up. He was glad to see that Anna wasn't too offended by his unfortunate choice of words. "That's too bad. I'm sure they'd enjoy it."

She didn't laugh as he expected, instead she picked up her briefcase. "I think we should take this walk so I quit saying stupid stuff."

"Aw, c'mon. Don't stop on my account," Chase said. "Usually I'm the one saying stupid stuff. It's nice to hear someone else do it for a change." He grabbed his cellphone and motioned towards the elevator. "After you, ma'am."

She sent him a smile and walked ahead of him. Chase watched her ass move under her skirt and couldn't deny that he wanted to get his hands on it. Anna was built the way women were meant to be, at least in Chase's estimation. Her voluptuous figure, creamy skin, and vibrant emerald eyes drew him like a bee to honey.

Not to mention her lustrous auburn hair. He'd like to take some pictures of her lying naked on his bed with her hair spread out over the pillows. *Hmm. I'm gonna make that happen.* However, he hadn't missed the wariness in her eyes and his male intuition told him that it would take more effort than usual to make that thought become a reality.

Her indifference just made him want her even more.

Anna was different. She hadn't flirted with him, or come on to him, when he'd turned down her designs. In fact, his world renown charm didn't appear to be working.

However, there was business to conduct first. So, he told his dick to behave and whistled to Lola to follow them. They boarded the elevator and Chase hit the button for the twelfth floor.

"So what was your favorite thing to eat at the Diner?"

A blush spread across Anna's cheeks. "Oh, lots of different things."

"Which tells me that you're the kind of woman I like best."

Her startled eyes met his. "And what kind is that?"

"The kind with an appetite. I hate women who sit and pick over a salad and pretend that they're full after three bites. Irritates the shit out of me," Chase said. "The Triple Decker cheeseburger, fries, coleslaw, and a large chocolate shake was my favorite meal, which I ate before every game."

Bashfully, Anna said, "I tried to tackle a Triple Decker a couple of times, but I couldn't finish it."

Chase patted her shoulder. "Don't worry about it. You tried and that's all that counts. Right, Lola?"

Lola barked and blinked at Chase.

"Does she go everywhere with you?"

"Yeah, except for in the cafeteria. Health regulations. Other than that, she's allowed everywhere. Lola is good for my soul," Chase said softly.

"She's beautiful."

Anna was beautiful. Her smile drew Chase's attention back to her luscious mouth and he wanted to shove her up against the wall and kiss her until they were both breathless and—not a good idea to mix business and pleasure but then hell, he never played by the rules.

The elevator stopped and they exited it.

"This floor is what I call the War Room," Chase said. "Just a warning: it's pretty messy."

He opened the door directly across from the elevator and a cacophony of noise poured forth. The sounds of people typing on keyboards and copiers running mixed in with loud voices and blaring music.

"What's going on in here?" Anna asked.

Chase grinned mysteriously. "You'll see."

As he escorted Anna into the War Room, Chase kept things fun and casual, but he was already thinking of how he was going to charm the gorgeous woman from his hometown into bed.

Did you enjoy Love Me?

If you'd like to support Bronwen Evans's work here's how you can help:
(ps: Bronwen also has Bron's Bold Belles. To learn how you can become part of her team and win a trip to New Zealand to meet her, visit www.bronwenevans.com/street-team/)
1. Loan this book to your friends.
2. Buy Bron's next book during the first week of release. Sign up for her newsletter (and receive a FREE eBook) so you'll be in the know.
3. Tweet/Share that you finished this book and consider sharing a link to Bron's website.
4. Mention the book on blogs that ask what you're reading. If you discover Bron is blogging someplace, be sure to pop by and leave a comment.
5. Visit and like Bron's Facebook page.
6. Or simply send Bron an email: bronwen@bronwenevans.com

Thanks so much for your support!

Discover More by Bronwen Evans

The Disgraced Lords
A Touch of Passion
A Whisper of Desire
A Taste of Seduction
A Night of Forever
A Love to Remember

Wicked Wagers
To Dare the Duke of Dangerfield
To Wager the Marquis of Wolverstone
To Challenge the Earl of Cravenswood

Invitation To
Invitation to Ruin
Invitation to Scandal
My Lord's Invitation to Passion
Invitation to Pleasure
Invitation to Sin
Invitation to Love

Imperfect Lords
Addicted to the Duke

Coopers Creek (contemporary)
Love Me
Heal Me

Other Books
The Reluctant Wife (contemporary)

About the Author

USA Today bestselling author, Bronwen Evans grew up loving books. She writes both historical and contemporary sexy romances for the modern woman who likes intelligent, spirited heroines, and compassionate alpha heroes. Evans is a three-time winner of the RomCon Readers' Crown and has been nominated for an RT Reviewers' Choice Award. She lives in Hawkes Bay, New Zealand with her dogs, Brandy and Duke.

Bronwen loves hearing from avid romance readers at Bronwen@bronwenevans.com.

You can keep up with Bronwen's news by visiting her website www.bronwenevans.com
Or Facebook: https://www.facebook.com/bronwenevansauthor
Or Twitter: https://twitter.com/bronwenevans_NZ

Read. Feel. Fall in Love.

Printed in Great Britain
by Amazon